Fríða Ísberg is an Icelandi[c] books are the poetry colle[ction] *Jacket Weather*, the short s[tory] *The Mark*, which won the Fjara Literature Prize, the Icelandic Booksellers Award, and the P. O. Enquist Award. Ísberg is the 2021 recipient for the Optimist Award, awarded by the President of Iceland to one national artist. Her work has been translated into seventeen languages.

Further praise for *The Mark*:

'Gripping ... In a series of gradually intertwining plotlines, *The Mark* presents crucial ethical questions about the risks of social engineering and the boundaries of individual agency.' Hernan Diaz

'Ísberg has written a masterpiece of public conscience and consciousness. *The Mark* moves in propulsive prose, between four main characters so singular and human and fallible, I feel I could pick up my phone right now and call any of them ... One of the most fascinating and ethically nourishing contemporary novels I've read in ages.' Kaveh Akbar

'A compelling and deeply intelligent novel ... Notions of vulnerability and belonging are beautifully rendered, while never disregarding the fear and hypocrisy that can shadow them. Ísberg has crafted a novel with razor-sharp insight and deliciously dark humour.' Rijn Collins

'Like the best dystopian fiction *The Mark* arrives at the perfect moment ... *The Mark* speaks directly to the here-and-now.' *Herald*

'A very human story about a few individuals trying in different ways to live their lives under conditions that become increasingly absurd.' *Vi Magazine* (Sweden)

'A novel that tells us more about our present than the future.' *Deutschlandfunk Kultur* (Germany)

'A dystopian thesis novel that illuminates the dark side of our omnipresent desire for empathy [...] In addition to being an allegory of state and digital surveillance in the context of the pandemic, *The Mark* also provides a specific critique of the empathic praise of empathy in the age of psychology.' *WELT plus* (Germany)

'[Ísberg] does not only address existential questions on power and morality with intuition and wisdom but also tackles language and style with great and captivating vigour.' *Skáld* (Iceland)

'Dystopic and elegant [...] Ísberg has an original and totally immersive take on what an emerging, totalitarian society may do to fully fleshed-out, utterly believable people ... very timely.' *Adresseavisen* (Norway)

Fríða Ísberg

The Mark

Translated by
Larissa Kyzer

faber

First published in 2024
by Faber & Faber Ltd
The Bindery, 51 Hatton Garden
London EC1N 8HN

First published in Icelandic in 2021 as *Merking* by Forlagið

This paperback edition first published in 2025

Typeset by Faber & Faber Ltd
Printed in the UK by CPI Group (UK) Ltd, Croydon CR0 4YY

A CIP record for this book
is available from the British Library

ISBN 978-0-571-37676-6

MIX
Paper | Supporting
responsible forestry
FSC
www.fsc.org   FSC® C013604

Printed and bound in the UK on FSC® certified paper in line with our continuing
commitment to ethical business practices, sustainability and the environment.
For further information see faber.co.uk/environmental-policy

Our authorised representative in the EU for product safety is
Easy Access System Europe, Mustamäe tee 50, 10621 Tallinn, Estonia
gpsr.requests@easproject.com

2 4 6 8 10 9 7 5 3 1

In the end, everything turns out somehow,
doubtful though it may seem at the time.

Halldór Laxness, *Independent People*

Laíla,

Why must all of our conversations always go down the same path? Why is it so impossible for us to have a discussion without it devolving into a question of my opinion? I'm not convinced of anything. All I wanted was to consider both sides of the matter, to see if both perspectives held water. I hate this no-man's-land. I hate that society is always splitting into two warring armies defending their trenches, that anyone who ventures into the middle gets shot down by both sides. (Oh, and while I'm at it: 'politics' doesn't mean 'polar opposites', as you'd have it. The word 'politics' is rooted in the Greek concept of 'politeia', which means 'affairs of the state'.)

This is not – and should not be – 'you're either with us or against us'. North Pole or South.

I wasn't rationalising anything. All I was trying to say is that when geese fly in V-formation, it reduces wind resistance and makes it easier for the whole flock to migrate. When one goose flaps its wings, there's an updraught that benefits the bird behind it. If a bird drops out of formation, it has to fight a stronger headwind, so, naturally, it hurries back in line. The flock sticks together because it's advantageous to do so, because it betters all the birds' chances of survival. But this doesn't change the fact that flying in V-formation requires a social hierarchy, each according to their abilities. The strongest birds fly in the front, cleaving through the wind for the others. The further back a bird is, the easier its journey. Easiest of all would be to fly in the middle of the V, but that would never be tolerated – because such a bird wouldn't be contributing to the flock's overall goals. The others would start squawking immediately.

In saying this, I didn't mean that psychopaths – and sorry, I refuse to bow to this inane, politically correct demand that we call them 'people with moral disorders' – are the strongest birds. As a rule, a psychopath makes it look like they're flying at the head of the formation, when really, they're flying in the middle of the V. A psychopath isn't the strongest bird, they're the weakest link. (There's an extra layer of ambiguity here in Icelandic, of course, as we use the same word, *veikur*, to mean both 'weak' and 'ill'. We conflate these dichotomies: strong and weak, healthy and ill. So when we talk about weak links – individuals who are not working for Icelandic society as a whole – we are literally writing them off as ill.)

This reminds me, of course, of Nietzsche. The difference between good and evil, good and bad. You're probably rolling your eyes right now, but this is important. According to society's moral barometer, attributes that serve the whole (solidarity, helpfulness) are 'good', while attributes that threaten the whole (selfishness, amorality) are 'evil'. And this, of course, is counter to what we all intuitively feel: 'What's good for me is good, what's bad for me is bad.'

But as a group (a flock, a society), we've now started to conflate strength and psychopathy. As a result, certain human attributes that have long been associated with strength – testosterone and assertiveness, for instance – are not only shameful flaws, but straight-up symptoms of disease. Which is like saying that knives are flaws, are symptoms. Sure, knives can be dangerous – how many people have been killed by knives? And yet we use them every single day, in every kitchen in the world.

I get how this happened, of course: we've long disparaged concepts like open dialogue and humility. But then what becomes of those birds that really are strong, the ones who cleave through the wind for the rest? Just look at Alþingi, at what's happened since the marking mandate came into effect for all of parliament. Now the nation knows – beyond a shadow of a doubt – that no MP is clinically psychopathic; we can no longer sweep politicians into one big rubbish pile of corruptness whenever we see fit. And yet, all of them have continued to speak in silver-tongued riddles. No one dares be direct because assertiveness is now the same thing as violence.

So it goes. Our definitions of words expand and contract, deviate and intertwine. Utensils become murder weapons and strengths become weaknesses. All depending on the context.

All this being said, I do want to take a step back and apologise for taking my leave yesterday. But you should know by now how I get when my back is against a wall – when someone tells me I've got to agree with political correctness or else I'm a bad person. Let me breathe, Laíla. Let me mull this over for myself without calling me a wolf in sheep's clothing. It isn't fair to turn philosophical speculations into personal accusations. If we're going to be friends for another twenty years, then we've got to be able to have a conversation without everything turning into attack and defence, shock and awe, fire and ash.

Tea

1.

Vetur is on her way to work when she gets a glimpse of a dark-haired man in the neighbourhood coffeehouse and there's something about his stiff shoulders that's enough to set her off all over again. She manages to make it past the corner, out of sight of the coffeehouse, before her legs go weak, her arms won't move, everything becomes too sharp, the colours too bright, the minor details too big. *Heart rate one hundred and eighty one beats per minute,* Zoé beeps, and the same feeling washes over her again: he's following her, he knows where she works, he's back at it, she has to hide. Someone comes up and asks if she's okay and she doesn't hear the voice until long after the words have been spoken; it takes her for ever to absorb their meaning, and she says Yes, she's fine, she tells Zoé not to sound the alarm, the last thing she wants is for the sirens to start wailing like last time. She exhales, inhales, exhales again. He can't get in here. He can't get into this neighbourhood. That couldn't have been him. And thinking about it now, the guy didn't look anything like Daníel, that guy was clean-cut and wearing a nice blazer, like someone who belongs in this neighbourhood, like someone who can get into this neighbourhood.

She's doubled over with her hands on her knees. She

straightens up and puts one foot in front of the other, heads towards the school as quickly as she can. She goes directly to her classroom and tries to calm down. By the time the first student walks in, she's stopped trembling. By noon, she has almost forgotten the whole thing.

After classes are over for the day, a representative from PSYCH, the Icelandic Psychological Association, comes in to talk to the teaching staff about how to prepare students. Experience has shown that it is best to play the test down a little, he says, to show them it's no big deal. Otherwise, they tend to blow it out of proportion.

'So how exactly are we supposed to spin this for them? Tell them it's some kind of treat?' asks Húnbogi, palms out in front of him, which, Vetur thinks, is about as close as you can get to throwing up your hands without actually throwing up your hands.

The representative tilts his head and thinks for a moment.

'No,' he says, his voice measured. 'Not a treat. But the closer we get to the referendum, the more cases we're seeing of young people who can't sleep due to test anxiety. Perhaps the adults in their homes are trying to form their own opinions about the marking mandate and don't realise that their children are like sponges, soaking up all that tension and uncertainty with very little context. Which is why we think it's important to call it a "sensitivity assessment" when dealing with individuals under eighteen years of age. Not an "empathy test". The language we use is important. We don't want young people to get the feeling that this is something they can fail. We're not marking anyone.'

The representative, Ólafur Tandri Sveinbjörnsson, is probably a little older than Vetur, somewhere between thirty and forty. He's often PSYCH's media spokesperson. The headmaster requested him specifically. Vetur understands why this man has been so successful in his field. There's something unassuming about him, something straightforward. If he were a house, he'd be built on rock. Not on sand like the rest of them.

'We're hoping these measures will forestall anxiety, dysphoria, shame, and even bullying. As teachers, you know better than anyone, of course, that this is a sensitive age, an age when individuals fall prey to herd mentality, when most of us want to fit in with the group. Your students will never see the results of their assessments. If need be, we'll be in touch with their form class leaders directly, but we identify very few problematic cases in marked schools, usually only in children who show clear signs of distress – trauma or neglect.'

'Excuse me, sorry,' says someone. Vetur sees it's one of the mothers on the parents' council. 'Are you saying that parents won't be informed which students fail and which students pass?'

'That's up to the school board,' says Ólafur Tandri. 'But we need to tread carefully. If a child is diagnosed below the norm, we need to take particular care with them. So, on that level, it would be logical for other parents to be informed. It takes a village, you know? But the danger then is that parents might unconsciously keep their kids away from the sick child and that would run counter to the whole point of the assessment. Antisocial behaviour needs to be met with social integration. If an assessment resulted in further isolation, we'd just be throwing the child out of the frying pan and into the fire.'

'Something like that would never happen in this neighbourhood,' answers the mother.

'We should hope not,' says Ólafur Tandri.

'What happens if a child is diagnosed below the norm?'

'If the assessors believe there's cause to intervene, they'll be in touch with the headmaster and the form class leader, and together, they'll offer appropriate resources to the parents.'

Vetur hurries out ahead of her co-workers. A few of the upper-division students are standing at the entrance; two of them are leaning against a wall, eating apples, a trend she can't fathom. She cuts across the schoolyard, past the transparent, plexiglassed football pitch. She walks quickly; she'd said she was going to the theatre when a colleague suggested going to 104.5, the coffeehouse on the border of the 104 and 105 postcodes where she'd thought she'd seen Daníel this morning. Why? Why does she do these things to herself? Someone had then asked what play she was going to see, and she'd said she wasn't sure, she was going with her mum, and it was a surprise. Anxiety feeds on lies. Now she has to remember to check what's showing tonight so she can answer questions on Monday.

She can't be bothered with the conversations people have after these kinds of meetings. Can't be bothered listening to her co-workers agreeing on fundamentals but disagreeing about trivialities, can't be bothered keeping her mouth shut while she listens to arguments she's heard a thousand times and then counterarguments she's heard a thousand times, can't be bothered walking the tightrope between wanting to say something and nothing to Húnbogi and then saying something to Húnbogi, who she can't be bothered to have a crush on but still does have a crush on because he's cute and somehow that lethal combination of knowing it and not knowing it, and when she thinks about him in the abstract, he's like a layer cake of alternating confidence and insecurity, and she can't be bothered to deal with that, either, although thinking about someone in the abstract is, of course, an entirely different thing from the tremor that shoots through her unexpectedly, the almost physical draw that pulls at her without warning, not to mention the self-consciousness and clumsiness and jokes that miss their marks.

She can hear a child crying in one of the apartments above. There's water running from a kitchen tap, plates clattering, and Vetur catches the savoury scent of someone's dinner wafting on the breeze. The pavement is bare – there are no weeds here, no cracks, the trees are as-yet only scrawny saplings. The eastern half of the neighbourhood, the part that's closest to the old industrial harbour, is still under construction; during the day, the sound of machinery carries into her classroom. But the western half is more or less finished – its white streets designed in a classic European style, tall buildings rising on either side like rows of perfectly straight teeth. The Viðey Quarter, located on the east side of Reykjavík and named after the island of Viðey just offshore, is the only marked neighbourhood in the downtown area. The other marked neighbourhoods are each at a similar stage of completion; one is located northeast of the city in a reforested area, the other on the coast, about half an hour to the south-west.

If they renew her contract at the end of the semester, she'll sell her apartment on Kleppsvegur and buy in the Viðey Quarter instead. It's the only way.

Soon Vetur catches sight of the thirty-foot glass wall, silvery and transparent, which encircles the neighbourhood. The wall ascends even higher at the end of the street, becoming a convex gate that faces the ocean and the thoroughfare that runs along the coast. This is gate one of two – the other is further up the hill at the other end of the neighbourhood. When Vetur was a teenager, there were some big warehouses here, but after they suffered major water damage it was decided the land would be elevated and the capital area enclosed, girded from the sea with the same plexiglass, all the way from Mt Esja north of the city to the lava fields in the south. 'The Glassworks', the media dubbed the project, but everyone else just calls it the levee.

When Vetur approaches the gate, one door slides open automatically, then back into place as soon as she steps past. She stands for a moment in the high-walled passage while the camera finds her face in the Registry. Then a second door slides open and she steps out.

Fear is a downwards motion, like sand in an hourglass. She double-checks that Chaperone is turned on, which, of course, it is. The heels of her shoes click on the pavement and betray her change of pace, her acceleration. This isn't how she sees herself. She's a scamp, she's a mischief-maker, she's devil-may-care. She's the type of person who isn't afraid to kill spiders in the bathtub, who isn't afraid to cook with ingredients that are long past their expiration date. She's not the type who has panic attacks in public or who needs gates to feel safe, not the type who's terrified to walk unmarked streets and has to check twice, three times, to make sure the door is locked before getting into bed.

Her psychiatrist says she's lucky. That she comes from a solid family and has a strong social network, and, as a result, should be able to work through this trauma fairly quickly. She's encouraged Vetur to be open with her people – her family and friends and co-workers – so as to forestall isolation, a common symptom of PTSD. Vetur has conscientiously heeded this advice, except when it comes to her new colleagues at the school, because PTSD can lead to a temporary loss of empathy in the sufferer, and in this neighbourhood, a loss of empathy is something that will impact a person's reputation, their livelihood.

A few weeks ago, late one night, someone rattled her doorknob. In an instant, it was all happening again, the hourglass flipped, and she ran to make sure the curtains were drawn, surveyed every square metre of the apartment to convince herself he hadn't got in, peeked through the heavy blinds over and over again to reassure herself that the black Benz wasn't outside. Even though she knew full well that Spotter and the restraining order would prevent him from getting within two hundred metres of her. Spotter would have notified the police immediately.

'Is your apartment building marked?' was their first question when she called. When she said no, they sent a car.

It was probably just a burglar, but every time she remembers the jangling doorknob, she imagines Daníel on the other side of the door. In his black parka, his bare hands cold and pink. Reminding her: she'll never be free of him.

She brought the petition up with the president of the co-op board yet again, but he just sighed and said that the old man on the third floor was still opposed to marking the building. Last time the president asked, the old coot had thundered that they could all just bide their time until he kicked the bucket, thank you very much, but Vetur doesn't have time to bide; the old man is only seventy or so, he easily has ten, maybe fifteen years left, if not more. And even if the building were marked, that wouldn't mean the whole complex or street would be. That could take years, decades even, if it were ever done at all. All that marking the building would mean is that unmarked people couldn't get past the face scanner in the main entrance. But hypothetically, fewer burglars would be able to rattle her doorknob.

She crosses the car park, unlocks the building's front door.

Once she's inside her apartment, she turns off Chaperone. She flops on to the sofa, asks Zoé to call her psychologist. *There is currently a two-week wait,* says a soft AI voice; her psychologist is at home this week with a sick child and not meeting with patients. After accepting an appointment in two weeks, Vetur sighs despondently and checks her social media. Her co-workers are all at 104.5. For a split second, she wants to run back there and elbow her way in between Húnbogi and the other Icelandic teacher so they won't be able to have any highbrow intellectual conversations that might lead to them becoming a highbrow intellectual couple, but then she imagines herself as part of just such a highbrow intellectual couple with Húnbogi and cringes at the thought.

Attempting to have a casual fling when you're on the verge of thirty-two is more trouble than it's worth, it inevitably collapses under the weight of looming questions about children and marriage and politics. But she isn't afraid of Húnbogi. She trusts him. Which is notable, given another side effect of the incident with Daníel: she's now afraid of men; sees something cruel in them. And it isn't just men she's afraid of, but also heart attacks and cancer and cars and aeroplanes; she's afraid for her family members and friends, afraid of getting bad news when the phone rings, afraid that someone has been diagnosed with a disease or wound up in an accident. This isn't how she sees herself. She's a scamp, she's a mischief-maker, she's devil-may-care.

She looks around. A year ago, this same living room was bathed in bright sunlight. Now, the late-afternoon sun is filtered through her yellow curtains. Vetur feels a lump in her throat. She closes her eyes and mourns her old life, back when she didn't feel like her every footstep was being followed. If she focuses, that feeling comes back to her and it's freedom – an endless, childlike freedom; she'd been seeing an attractive woman who'd just dumped her, and she was relieved. Vetur had known from the beginning that the relationship wasn't her final destination and she'd started revealing her worst side – strategically – so the attractive woman would lose interest, which mercifully, she did. When Vetur started her new job, she immediately scoped out her next prospect. The job was a one-year position while the regular social studies teacher was on maternity leave, Vetur had never taught before, had never been around teenagers in any real way. She'd spent a year trying to make a living as an ethicist, but that meant having a PhD in order to get grants and research projects and adjunct teaching gigs. But she didn't want to get a PhD or become an academic; she wanted to do something useful. Sit on committees, write articles, be asked her opinion, have a direct impact on society. Even though she got a few projects here and there and her CV was starting to look more like that of an adult, she was very often very broke and when the school advertised the temp position, it seemed like a perfect opportunity to shore up some funds and take a detour, an intermission.

It only took her a few days to zero in on the computer teacher. He was silent and skinny, wore nondescript clothes, had a scraggly beard and hair that had just started to abandon him. He didn't introduce himself, he never went to meetings or on staff outings, and he called in sick three days a month, like clockwork. She'd met guys like him in her philosophy courses, dark horses, and there was something in her subconscious that longed for a man like that, for undivided attention and simple adoration after her relationship with the attractive woman had become comfortable and flat like always, once her victory was assured and her euphoria dissipated, once she'd gnawed the fantasy of a new person down to the quick.

It didn't take much, just a few glances to reel him in, a question here and there over a couple of weeks to get him talking, the occasional conversation at the coffee machine to lure him out for a drink after work. He had dark eyes, knew a lot about politics and movies and music. He had a tendency to break into a little smile-laugh, sheepish, something more than a smile, but less than a laugh, and when it happened, lovely furrows appeared at the corners of his eyes and mouth. When they slept together, at her place, he was entirely passive and unassertive; she had to kiss him, lead him into the bedroom, undress him, undress herself, get protection, ask what position, and in the morning, she saw what she'd been hoping for: the face of a man who didn't believe what had happened, who couldn't believe his eyes, and it filled her with a particular kind of intoxication she hadn't felt in a long, long time.

2.

He says her name. Twice.

His voice calms her. Its baritone, its decisiveness. Which is funny considering how often that same decisiveness tried to nail her down.

Tried! Did not succeed.

'Will you come over?' she asks.

He gives her some excuse.

'I didn't ask if you had to wake up early, I asked if you'd come over,' she says.

He's turned off the camera. She tries turning it on again. He's asking her something.

Halló, she hears him saying. He says her name for the third time.

'*Já*, já, já, já, já. Yes. I'm here. Why won't you look at me?' she asks.

He says they were already in bed, he says it in a deep-voiced, serious whisper so she'll know she's crossed a line.

He says this can't go on any longer.

'I know,' she says.

He says he's going to block her.

'Breki. No. You can't do that to me,' she says.

'I love you,' she says.

Eyja, he says then. Goddamn it, Eyja.

He says he's not going to do this with her.

'Please. I can't take it,' she says.

He says something dramatic. Something about 'reaping what you sow'. Something about what she is.

'And you know what you are?' she asks.

'You're a jackhammer, Breki.'

'A jack that does nothing but hammer,' she says. 'And hammer, and hammer, and hammer.'

She hears the cow in the background. The cow is telling him to hang up.

'Is that the cow?' she says and laughs.

'COW,' she says with her face right up to the microphone. 'YOU ARE A COW.'

Breki says something, then something else and hangs up.

She tries calling again. He doesn't answer. She holds her wrist up to her face and records a gram. 'Remember, Breki, darling: cows don't spawn children. They spawn more cows.'

She tells Zoé to call Þórir.

It goes to voicemail. It's not that late.

What time is it?

Only eleven. Forty-five.

She leaves a gram for him, too.

She knew exactly what was up as soon as she saw him in the office today.

It only took her a fraction of a second to decipher the

guilty expression on his face, almost a grimace, the awkwardness in his voice.

The audacity of it – how could he even look her in the eye?

He said she was being let go, but that it was more of a provisional, six-month probation. She could take the test again after six months but, until then, she'd be under supervision.

Supervision.

Her.

No, she had to understand what a difficult position this put *him* in.

How hard this was on *him*.

He'd see to it that she got the best psychological treatment on offer.

He had no doubt that the treatment would be successful. That he'd be able to reinstate her in her job, take her off probation.

And if she failed the test a second time, after she'd gone through the rehabilitation process, they'd smooth things over by saying she'd quit of her own accord.

The way he'd rubbed his palms together when he said that if it were up to him, everyone would get the benefit of the doubt. But she had seen the numbers. There was nothing to do but to mark the company.

She just looked at him, his slack mouth and sunken eyes, his dark hair streaked with grey.

She imagined him in bed with his wife, thinking about her.

She knew he wanted her like that. But didn't dare make a move.

Not unless he was blind drunk in a different country.

And that's exactly what happened. The minute she rejected him, he ordered the test. The minute she told him through the hotel door to leave her alone, he ordered the test.

He got nervous when she mentioned that.

Sat up straight and said her name, said she shouldn't play this game, said she knew very well it wasn't like that. Gave her a pleading look. A look that was meant to say he didn't want to go to war.

'It's no wonder someone wouldn't pass the test after having been subjected to years of emotional abuse,' she said.

'That she'd have PTSD,' she said.

'Due to psychological violence,' she said.

'At the hands of her employer.'

Þórir held up his hands, like he was warding off a crazed bull.

Said he was on her side.

Said he would do whatever he could to help her.

To overcome this illness.

Every time he used that word, 'illness', she wanted to scratch his face off.

She told him what he was.

She told him what she was going to do.

He leaned back like she was a wasp about to sting him and she realised she'd jumped to her feet. He said something about first-rate companies and that she should think twice before she started rallying the troops and made a bad situation worse by taking retaliatory measures.

'Retaliatory measures,' she said. 'Retaliatory measures.'

'You might think in terms of revenge and betrayal and lies, Þórir,' she said. 'But don't try to paint the rest of us with the same shit-smeared brush.'

Þórir hung his head and, for a moment, she thought she'd won. But then his head started shaking and she saw he was laughing. Laughing like she'd said something funny – hysterical, even. She grabbed a gold-plated pen cup off his desk and threw it at the wall. Þórir shouted something at her as she stormed out.

She scrolls through her friend list. Stops at a guy who once tried to get her up to his hotel room.

Gylfi.

Perfect.

She texts him.

Zoé pings when the message is sent.

She peers at his profile picture. Closes one eye to see it better. It's a studio portrait, black-and-white; he's wearing a suit and has just the faintest, *faintest*, trace of stubble on his cheeks.

It's lickable, that stubble. Very lickable.

The next photo is of him with his family.

Three kids!

Blond, like their mum. His hair is dark.

She stands up and refills her glass. Sits back down. There's another ping from Zoé.

He says he's at someone's fiftieth. Says he can drop by in an hour.

She puts on better underwear and a dark blue dress and touches up her make-up. Vamps a little in the mirror.

She's still sexy. They can't take that away from her.

She hides the empty bottle but leaves the half-finished one on the table.

He's glassy-eyed when he arrives. A sweet scent of after-shave, a few buttons unbuttoned, she counts them, one, two, three, unbuttons a fourth one, a fifth.

His tongue is way too wet.

Slimy, like an octopus.

She turns her head away, hoping he'll kiss her somewhere else.

He's too loud, a heavy breather, and he groans and mumbles between kisses. It wrenches her out of the moment.

She hadn't noticed until now, for instance, that they were on the sofa.

'Hush,' she says. He laughs. She covers his mouth.

He says something into her palm and her palm moistens with his breath.

She wipes it on his shirt. Stands up and goes into the bed-room.

He follows and sits on the bed.

'Take your clothes off,' she says. She tries to unbutton her dress, stumbles into the door frame.

He's undressed and waiting. She asks him to help her.

He unbuttons her dress and pulls it down. She turns around and looks at him sitting on the bed.

He's squarish, beefy, his penis is squashed up against his belly, red and swollen.

None of this aligns with the chest hair and the unbuttoned shirt, both of which were so promising. He honks one of her breasts like a plush toy. Clumsily. Aggressively. His tongue's all over the place.

'Be still. Jesus.' She pushes him down and wonders if it might be worth tying him up, but he'd probably like it too much.

She straddles him, draws her underwear to the side.

And they're off.

Within a minute, he's breathing too shallowly.

'Wait. Stop. Stop, I said.' She climbs off him and holds him at arm's length when he tries to climb on top of her.

He laughs. Drags her underwear off. Asks what's the matter when she holds him off with her feet.

'You've got to last longer.'

He pretends he's offended. Or maybe he is offended. When he calms down a little, she pulls him back to her and he pants and moans and comes inside her.

She leaves him in the damp bedroom.

The night is empty. She tells her car to drive east on Sæbraut, along the levee, to turn into Laugarnes, the neighbourhood along the shore.

Sockless in her shoes, she's clenching a bottle of perfume

23

and her keys as she gets out, wobbling in front of the apartment building.

The cow's name is already on the goddamn mailbox. Like they're a family.

Like Breki didn't *just* leave her.

The divorce barely settled.

The ink still wet on the goddamn papers.

She can never remember which floor he lives on.

First floor, second floor, first floor, second floor?

They never spent much time here, in the early days. They always stayed over at hers.

Even after he moved in, he refused to sell his old apartment.

And then they got married, and he still refused to sell.

And then he moved out and took everything he owned – except the spare keys.

First floor. She drops the keys and has to fumble around for them on the carpet. Sticks the smaller one in the lock.

It doesn't work: second floor.

She gropes her way up a flight in the dark and the key slips smoothly into the lock.

It's one of those old-fashioned gold doorknobs.

She opens the door slowly. Slowly, just a crack, onto the vestibule where their coats are hanging.

She holds the perfume bottle up to the collar of his overcoat and spritzes. Then withdraws her hand, closes the door slowly behind her. Ever so slowly. And slips back out into the night.

—

She tells her car to stop at the Sun Voyager statue on the way home and gets out.

She can hear the surf crashing on the other side of the levee. The highwater mark is almost knee-level. The plexiglass crests over the pavement like a breaking wave.

Þórir. Chief Executive Bastard Þórir.

Þórir the coward. Þórir the slimeball.

The man who's looked at her like a prize. Like sweets.

Licked his lips like a greedy child. Laughed at everything she says. Recommended her, promoted her. Invited her to lunch.

Dinner. Or out for a drink.

Leaned over the arm of the leather sofa and said: If only I weren't a married man.

She asked him not to go through with the marking.

So did Alli and Fjölnir. They didn't want to mark the company either.

But no. All the green companies wanted their investors to be marked, he said.

Which was nonsensical. There was only one company that opted to go with marked investors instead of them.

One.

But that was enough to throw Þórir into a panic. And convince the rest of the board.

And so there was nothing to do but to take the test.

Anything else would have been stupid.

And now she must be put down.

Now the vixen must be smoked from her burrow.

She looks into the camera on her right wrist, records another gram, and sends it to Þórir.

She looks out on the mass across the bay, Mt Esja, draped in darkness. She hopes the octopus will be gone when she gets back. Then her eyes fall on a black scrawl on the levee, right in front of her. She steps towards the transparent glass and squints.

MARK THEM ALL.

3.

On Thursday, yet another boy dies by his own hand. Twenty-two years old. On Friday, everything's a shambles. The boy's relatives say he had no hope for his future, that he failed the test when he was eighteen and after that, his life was marred by drug abuse and depression. On Saturday, the worst riot yet takes place. Around five thousand people gather outside Alþingi, the stone parliament house on Austurvöllur Square, and chant the boy's name. Most of them are peaceful, but on the front line it's all young men, some of whom are wearing holomasks, some of whom aren't. A few are armed with petrol bombs, others with fireworks. First, they spit and beat on the SWAT team's protective barrier, then they try to force their way into parliament. When they can't get in, the violence intensifies; windows are broken in the surrounding buildings, cars set aflame. One of the young men is seen driving into the square in a large pickup truck loaded with a hundred-litre tank of flammable liquid and empty glass bottles. He's immediately intercepted by police. Almost fifty people are arrested. Six are seriously injured, including one police officer, who ends up in intensive care with a fractured skull.

On Sunday, the nation is in shock. The prime minister condemns the actions as a failed insurrection. On Monday, the police officer dies from his injuries. The national commissioner honours the officer during a live broadcast on national TV with a minute of silence. On Tuesday morning, Ólafur Tandri drives past a billboard of himself on which someone has drawn Xs over his eyes. On Thursday, he goes out to find that his tyres have been slashed. He stands in front of the car, calls Himnar, and asks him to come and pick him up. He feels a cold wave of tension go through his body. He thinks: The car is fine. He thinks: Tyres are just tyres. But then, a few minutes later, he discovers that he also received a death threat in the middle of the night:

> next im going to put a bag over your fucking kids head and make you watch her suffocate and then im going to rape your wife and shoot you in the fucking head

It's the same anonymous account that has sent him all sorts of threats before, but this time the message was sent with a picture of his car and the tyres. That's what makes it feel truly invasive. He calls Salóme, Salóme calls the police. The police have promised them all Chaperone Plus until the referendum. He's not totally sure what that means, except that if he says 'nine' three times in a row – 'nine nine nine' – he'll be connected to a dispatcher. Other than that, they recommend that he and his colleagues travel to and from work together and never go out alone.

Sólveig doesn't say anything as the technician sets up the security system that night. Óli can feel her anger in every fibre of his being. He apologises when the technician leaves.

She busies herself taking care of Dagný, as she so often does when she can't bring herself to look at him.

PSYCH's head office isn't in a marked neighbourhood and it doesn't have a parking garage, either, which means that its employees are completely exposed as they walk from their cars to the entrance. The same is true of his home. Sólveig refuses to relocate to the Viðey Quarter – no matter what he says, she remains unmoved. He's grateful when Himnar suggests they carpool to work from now on.

Apart from the appearances he makes on behalf of the association, he's stopped going out in public. He doesn't even go to the grocery store if he can avoid it. When he picks up Dagný from preschool, the other parents give him encouraging smiles. Only once has someone tried to pick a fight with him, some random grandfather. Another parent was quick to come to Óli's defence and he hurried out as fast as he could, Dagný in his arms, her boots forgotten in the coatroom.

When he picks Óli up on Friday morning, Himnar is biting his nails and puffing the shreds onto the car seat. Óli closes his eyes and tries to relax, but each puff is like an assault on his nervous system. The team working on the referendum campaign starts each day with a meeting of the six of them. Salóme is standing at one end of the table. Óli counts five heads, asks who's missing. Himnar looks at him, clearly amused.

'You?'

Óli rubs his eyes, shakes his head, and laughs with his colleagues. He does this kind of thing a lot lately. Looks for something when he's holding it. Forgets words and names. Says 'epitome' when he means 'epiphany'. Trails off mid-sentence. He writes down what he's done every day because, by the next day, he'll have forgotten. He's burnt out.

'There is, however, one bright side to this tragedy,' Salóme is saying. 'As of this morning, according to the latest figures, it's sixty-five per cent in favour, twenty-one per cent opposed. That's a nine per cent jump in one week. People are coming around. They can see what needs to happen. Then there's also the matter of the interview Magnús Geirsson gave this morning.'

She projects a news clip. It shows the chairman of MASC, Men Against Social Compulsion, standing in front of a residential building on Hverfisgata, his expression one of concern tinged with grief. The death of the police officer is a shock to everyone, he says, and MASC sends its thoughts and prayers to the victim's family.

'Violence like this doesn't come out of nowhere,' he says to an offscreen reporter. 'These boys don't have a voice in society. This is their way of taking control, of getting their own back. Unfortunately. It's no coincidence that there is a wave of burglaries sweeping through the country or that we are breaking narcotics crime records left and right. Society is manifesting the danger it claims to be preventing.'

He cites a new survey that found that two out of every three young men have experienced 'moral prejudice'. Young men are given less of a chance, he explains: they're sent into treatment straight out of primary school and are hired for more menial jobs than girls. This gives girls a considerable advantage on the labour market. It isn't until around the age of twenty-five – when boys start testing at higher levels of emotional intelligence and girls start having babies – that the gender wage gap begins to even out. Around a fifth of young men under the age of twenty-five are neither in school nor employed. The riots on Saturday are a clear consequence of systemic discrimination.

They spend the rest of the morning hashing out bullet points for the media response. Firstly, they will not use the word 'death'. They're going to call this incident by its rightful name: 'murder'. The police officer was *murdered* on Saturday. Secondly, they're going to say that Saturday's riot is proof positive that these young men are in need of help and that the marking mandate is absolutely necessary. Thirdly, they'll point out that the city's crime rate has actually gone down, not up. There is no 'wave of burglaries' to speak of – burglaries are occurring at the exact same rate they have been for years. But these crimes have become more concentrated. Five years ago, there were burglaries all over the capital area, but after the introduction of marked neighbourhoods and marked hallways in residential buildings, there have, of course, been more break-ins in unmarked areas, the neighbourhoods that MASC supporters call home.

'Himnar, collate the burglary stats, would you, and Óli, you issue the response?' says Salóme.

'On it,' they say in unison.

—

31

Two hours later, Himnar sends him a clean draft of the response with the correct figures from the police.

'Did you get it?' he asks. They're sitting back to back.

'Yeah,' says Óli without looking up from his screen. He hears the rhythmic rustling of Himnar's trouser leg, vibrating like a hummingbird wing. Which means that Himnar's had too much coffee. Which means that Himnar has become sloppy. Óli tries not to let it irritate him, but it does. Himnar is always ignoring his own boundaries. Óli is looking forward to getting some space after the referendum. They've been working so much together that everything about his best friend is getting on his nerves: his ADHD, his disorganisation, his whistling. Although, admittedly, Óli's nerves are like an old sewage system these days. It doesn't take much for them to clog and overflow.

He tries to ignore the furore after the media publishes PSYCH's response. He tries not to look at people's comments. But as soon as he gets home, he gives in and reads everything. The fors, the againsts, the vilifications. He was told he'd get used to all the uproar, but he hasn't. Every time he gets a message from an imploring voice, pleading with him to put himself in their son's shoes, he has to convince himself all over again. Remind himself why he's doing what he's doing.

Ever since he was a teenager, he's known they could do better. He watched his friends ball up their fists, punch walls. He saw their jaw muscles bulge when they tried to keep their faces blank. He knew how they felt. The same rage welled up inside him from time to time, his ribcage expanding like the land on a tectonic plate boundary. He understood this sensation, the feeling that you couldn't contain all your anger. Sometimes, he clenched his jaw and pressed his lips together so that what was inside him wouldn't get out: if it did, he wouldn't be able to control it. He wouldn't be able to reel it back in.

He watched his father debate his mother half to death. He watched her hold her tongue, shake her head when she didn't have a response. He'd tell his dad not to talk to her like that and his dad would say, Like what? We're just having a conversation. His father didn't clench his fists or slam doors. But he interrupted, shook his head wearily, declared that actually, that was simply not correct – that unfortunately, things just don't work Like That, they work Like This. His father asserted when he was merely guessing. He explained in order to fill empty space. He was certain when he was unsure.

In a democratic society, revolution comes in waves, it comes from outside, it drips from the public into the government like rainwater through a roof. The key element isn't the rainwater, but the roof. A roof doesn't leak unless it needs to be replaced, and the old roof was leaking like a sieve. There was a major societal shift during Óli's first semester of sixth form, when the government began offering psychological services as part of the national mental-health system. Óli was allocated a weekly appointment with a psychologist on Tuesdays between French and biology and it was during these sessions that he learned to identify the feeling of turmoil he sometimes felt. His psychologist gave him the tools to talk to his father, to explain how his overbearing behaviour made his family feel. *When you talk like that, it makes us feel like this. When you use that tone, we get defensive.*

He watched his father work himself into a lather over all this whining about feelings. His sister shushing their father, telling him he could take his aggression and shove it, that if he wanted to be included in conversations, then he needed to act like a civilised human being. This wasn't a game of tug of war or a competition. He watched his father snap that they were all welcome to their tact and respect or whatever they wanted to call this echo chamber of theirs, this I-hear-what-you're-saying-but-I-feel-differently mollycoddling, but he was having none of it. He believed in freedom of speech and healthy confrontation.

Óli learned to read politicians the same way he read his father. He learned to be courteous and stay on an even keel. He got involved in university politics and refined his father's language. 'You need to check your facts' became 'I understand what you're saying, but have you thought about it this way?' He joined PSYCH's youth organisation, which lobbied for emotional intelligence – how to put themselves in someone else's shoes – from the moment they started their compulsory education at six until they finished secondary school at sixteen. At the time, the empathy test was only available within the mental-health system, as a measure of success for convicted criminals or other unwell individuals who were struggling 'with moral disorders'.

And then came the big data leak. Óli was twenty-two years old and had just fallen in love with Sólveig. They were allowed to leave class early so they could stand outside parliament with thousands of others, demanding resignations, day after day. He remembers those cold November days, alternately cloudless and overcast. He remembers slinging around words like 'narrative', 'criteria' and 'post-structuralism', remembers the smile on Sólveig's face when she saw through him. He remembers standing among those throngs of people and thinking that if human history had a heart, they were now within its beat. The moment in which the pendulum stops swinging mid-air, just for a second, before swinging back in the opposite direction.

There are conflicting stories as to where the idea came from. Some say the politician who fared the worst in the data leak suggested it, that in a gambit to restore his image, he said he would take the empathy test to disprove the popular notion that he was, in the clinical sense of the word, a psychopath. Some say the idea came from the public. One MP took her test results to the papers, then another. One political party announced that all its members would be tested, then another followed suit. Three weeks later, the majority of Alþingi voted in favour of a testing requirement for MPs, in hope of restoring public trust. Óli heaved a sigh of relief with the rest of the nation when seven MPs were forced to resign.

The next few years were spent strengthening the infrastructure of the mental-health system. Iceland's new government followed the example of its Nordic neighbours and invited members of the public to take the test free of charge, while also laying the foundation for the treatment options available to individuals who tested under the norm. 'We're investing in mental health,' said the minister of health, a sixty-three-year-old nurse who'd worked at the National University Hospital for three and half decades. 'And it's going to pay off for the entire nation.' She'd casually shared her results with her colleagues during a shift change at the hospital. Her results had been leaked and not long after, she'd been offered a cabinet post as a non-member of parliament.

The government conceded to the public's demand that testing be mandatory for law enforcement officers, as well as judges, cabinet members, and executive officials all the way up to the prime minister. Not long after, the City of Reykjavík decided that employees in caretaking positions must furnish certification of a passing score, and that emotional intelligence would be remunerated accordingly. Then, after an additional one and a half election cycles, people began clamouring for a public registry in which test-takers could voluntarily record their results. Falsified certificates sprouted up like chickweed, generally when people were applying for jobs, or apartments on the rental market. No one had talked about 'the mark' or 'marking yourself' until PSYCH made the Registry accessible to the public four years ago. When that happened, people were able to look each other up and see who had really passed the test.

Óli watched his father grow increasingly silent when he was not at home. At first, he'd bragged about being unmarked, but then he stopped. Every now and then, Óli would walk in on his father talking to friends on the phone, voice lowered and lamenting the state of the world. It was disgraceful, he'd say. Absolutely disgraceful.

Articles are now being published on a daily basis, explaining how the mark protected 'normal' people from 'broken' people and how many of those same broken people had either moved out of the country or gone into treatment and improved. Óli experiences the same sense of relief each time; one more tiny tangle has been combed from the great mane of society.

He's about to turn off Zoé and start cooking dinner when he notices that his inbox is blinking.

fuck you fucking emotional sluts were going to kill you all

4.

Fucking goddamn pieceofshit fucking hell. Tristan tries to fast-forward. He tries to stop. But it's another one of those fucking videos that Zoé makes you watch. He tries to breathe through it, but the words force their way into his skull and fucking rape his ears, tell him life doesn't have to be hard, that he doesn't need to bear the burden alone, but THEY are the ones who are making his life hard, THEY are the ones who are creating the burden. One minute you're playing CityScrapers on the S-line and then suddenly the game stops and an ad comes on and their voices start blasting in your ears and then you're just so fucking angry and the day is fucking ruined.

Like the other day: he was on the way home from work and he'd just got another No from some company that didn't even give him the fucking chance to come in for a fucking interview and then fucking Ólafur Tandri popped up and told him he should take the test and he just lost it, he went straight home and wrote down everything he was thinking, like literally EVERYTHING, sent it off, and then he waited until midnight, grabbed a little kitchen knife, and went out . . .

The S-line stops at Lækjartorg and he gets off. Everything's a mess after the protest, the grounds covered with rubbish and fireworks and broken glass. He hears heels clicking. It's a woman wearing one of those fur hats, she makes eye contact and then looks away way too fucking fast, she wraps her coat tighter around her and is he imagining it or does she start walking faster? No, he's definitely not imagining it. Chicks are a lot more afraid of him now that he's shaved his head, they turn on their watches so that if he gets anywhere near them sirens will go off and satellites will start recording them and some AI somewhere will track where he's going and report it to the cops. That's what Eldór says, but maybe it isn't true. How is an AI supposed to see through roofs? Thermal imaging? That would be classic Eldór, just talking out of his arse without doing his own research. Just running his mouth about all this sci-fi shit he thinks sounds good.

Like when he said the cops could see if you'd been speeding because new cars keep records of how fast you drive and then send it to them. And that cops pay car companies for your data.

Oh yeah? Tristan said, and then he'd repeated that all over town. They were always hearing stories about guys the cops picked up for no reason, they'd just drive up out of nowhere and shove these dudes in the back of a cop car. But of course Viktor and them just laughed in his face like he was fucking stupid and he said, Yeah, I'm serious, for real, that's what happens, and then when he asked Eldór where he heard it, Eldór said he just knew because they'd sent him a speeding ticket the other day and he was positive he hadn't driven by a single traffic cam.

Tristan tried to google, tried to understand data protection laws, he even asked Zoé to explain them to him, but the cops make laws so fucking confusing on purpose, sometimes they're allowed to check satellite footage and sometimes not, and so all this time since he slashed those fucking tyres, his stomach has been killing him, he walks past Ólafur Tandri's house every day and instead of feeling glad when he sees the car all hacked up in the driveway, he feels like someone is scooping out his stomach with a spoon, like he's a boiled egg being scraped out of its shell or something, and he imagines over and over that they will find some video in some database and figure out that Tristan lives only two minutes away.

He's busted his arse and paid his dues and saved up and counted every single fucking króna for over a year, he's been working like a motherfucker every day down at the harbour, eating frozen pizzas and sleeping on a mattress on the floor and checking his bank balance every single day but then that gives him panic attacks so he goes and breaks into some house, cleans it, gets some fast cash and has the money to buy real food and trex for a while and sometimes some other pills that make his stomach hurt way fucking worse, probably because he's so stressed about whether the cops are on to him and then he promises himself he's never ever going to clean again, never, and starts saving up again and eating frozen shit and obsessing over his bank account until he has another panic attack and cleans another house.

But then out of nowhere, right when he was about to give up, right when he was a hundred per cent sure he'd never make it: money. After the worst year of his life, after he dropped out of school to work so he could get an apartment and be safe, after he saw what could happen, after he saw how his life could turn out, suddenly: money.

He sees the sign for a corner store further down Hverfisgata. It's on the ground floor of Eldór's building.

'To Eldór,' he says into his watch. 'I'm here. Come down.'

His mouth feels like fucking sandpaper. He decides to get something to drink before they head out, but as soon as he steps towards the sliding door, an alarm goes off: EE EE EE. He looks up and sees a PSYCH sticker on the glass.

'What the fuck?' He looks in and sees a girl behind the register staring at him, dead-faced. 'You're joking,' he says, even though the girl can't hear him, of course. Last week, this shop wasn't marked. Now there's a second door after the first one, creating a little glass box at the entrance. Some middle-aged guy walks past him and the first door slides open. Out of nowhere Tristan feels this killer urge to jump into the box with the guy, to protest and wait in there for the cops, because the second door won't open unless you're by yourself, but he doesn't, he just watches as the first door swallows the guy and he stands there for a couple seconds before the second door opens and lets him go into the shop. Tristan takes a few steps away from the entrance. More people walk by, pretend they don't see him. He hears a soft click behind him and Eldór walks out.

'About fucking time, dude.'

'Sorry,' says Eldór as he grabs his hand, pulls him in, and claps him on the back.

'It's fucking cold.'

'Yeah, sorry, man, I was just, *þú veist*, you know, takin' care of business.'

'What's the deal with this?' asks Tristan, pointing at the shop.

'Some guy came in waving a knife and the owners marked it,' says Eldór. He points to a window in the back. 'They serve the unmarked from there.'

They walk down to the big hotel on Sæbraut. The girl behind the desk looks at them like they're going to do something and when he sees the look on her face Tristan wants to tell her to stop staring and judging and to give people a fucking chance. She's blond and her hair is pulled back into a really tight ponytail and she's got acne on her cheeks.

'Hey,' says Eldór. 'We're here to see Magnús Geirsson. Can you let us up?'

She looks back and forth between them like they said something offensive and Tristan looks at her neck and her neck reminds him of Sunneva, who hasn't answered him in like three months and all of a sudden he wants to say something that will make this girl feel better so he whispers 'She's cute' to Eldór while she's calling upstairs and he says it loud enough that she definitely hears him.

He's on the seventh floor, she says and then starts messing with something behind the desk and doesn't look at them again.

'These bitches, man,' says Eldór when the elevator closes.

'I hear you.'

'Bet she's one of those chicks who hate men, you know what I'm saying? Like HATES men. She was into it, though, I could tell.'

'What I said?'

'Yeah, she was trying not to smile.'

'Eh, I don't know, man. Chicks are all real fucking scared of me. Especially now I shaved my head,' he says, pointing.

'You just got to act all gentle, dude. Soft.'

Eldór makes a face that's supposed to be soft.

'Yeah, well, I don't want to go around with some bitch with zits all over her face anyway.'

'Zits?'

'Yeah, she had these huge pimples on her face, a bunch of them. Didn't you see?'

'Dude, no one notices that.'

'I do.'

They get out at the seventh floor and some guy says hi and tells them to sit on the couch by the window.

'They're just about ready.'

'Okay,' says Eldór.

Tristan can smell his own sweat. Now that he's here it doesn't matter that he took a whole trex, his heart is still racing like a mouse running from a fucking cat. Zoé says his heart rate is too high. He thinks of something Rúrik said to him once, way back. *Somehow, it all turns out somehow.* That author, the guy who won the prize, he said it. Good shit.

Tristan has never been interviewed before. He doesn't know anything about talking in front of a camera. They only went to that MASC meetup last weekend because the guy who hooks them up with trex said you got paid for going the first time so they went that night and both got cash and dinner and then they all sat in a circle and listened to the other guys talk about all the shit that had happened to them because of the test. It was weird listening to them – at first, he thought they were fucking dumbasses, admitting all the illegal shit they were admitting to, he was sure someone must be recording and sending all of it to the cops or something but then he just sort of forgot for all intensive purposes because the stuff they were saying was all stuff Tristan could have said himself. They could have been talking about him, so much of it was the exact fucking same, so when it was his turn to talk, he felt like they'd understand.

Which is why he told them about the time his mum announced that they were going to move into the marked neighbourhood and he said, What, you're going to fucking abandon me? And she said No, of course not, you'll just take the test, like it was no big deal and he said that fucking test destroyed his brother's life and then she said Tristan Máni Axelsson, you are going to take that test and we are going to move and I don't want to hear another word about it. So then he said Adios, bitch, and left wearing just a thin jacket and he called Rúrik and his brother told him that had been a stupid fucking thing to do and told him to go home and hung up on him. So then he called different friends he used

45

to hang out with and they all said *Nei*, sorry, when he asked if he could crash at their places. This was back around the time he'd just got hooked on trex and he wasn't working so he was always borrowing money from friends and never paid any of it back and once when he was desperate, he stole from one of them and then they all stopped talking to him.

He called his dad who lived in Spain and he was just like, I know it's hard, kid, but you got to go home, so then he finally called his dealer and that guy told him to come down to the harbour and Tristan walked all the way over there. The guy lived in this old warehouse that was abandoned because the sea had flooded it a bunch of times. There were tons of storage rooms on the top floor and when he walked down the hall, he saw all these guys who were his same age, all super fucking skinny, right, and some of the rooms had beds and couches and tables but most of them just had mattresses and rubbish and piles of clothes on the floor. When he knocked on the door of the guy he knew, two other dudes were there too and the guy he knew gave him a trex and said just pay him later and that he could crash on the couch which was disgusting and smelled like duck shit and after the other guys went to bed he was just lying there awake because he was sure he was going to get robbed if he fell asleep and a couple times he almost stood up and went home and agreed to take the fucking test and move into the fucking neighbourhood but then he imagined talking to his mum and got so fucking angry at how weak she always was, so fucking angry, and he just kept lying there one hour after another and that's how he passed the night until he finally fell asleep around sunrise.

When he woke up someone had taken both of his earbuds and his watch and so he didn't have Zoé and didn't know what time it was. He was supposed to be at school and he thought about going to class but instead he woke up the guy he knew and asked if he knew about any work or if maybe he could start dealing himself and then the guy he knew said that Viktor was always looking for solid guys and that same day he went down to the harbour and found Viktor and Viktor said okay and that evening some random dude picked him and a third guy up and they went and cleaned a house way out in the suburbs, they took fucking everything, like literally everything, clothes and kitchen shit and instruments and electronics and when they brought back the car Viktor paid him right then and asked if he'd be coming back tomorrow and Tristan said yeah. He slept at the warehouse again that night and kept the money from Viktor in his boxers.

Late that night he promised himself he would work like a motherfucker and get his own place so he'd never turn out like these guys. He slept on that couch for a month and a half and heard all sorts of disgusting shit through the walls and when he had finally saved enough for a security deposit, he found an apartment not far from the harbour. That first night was the best night of his life. For a whole week, he felt like he was safe and he applied for normal jobs and even went to school to see if he could finish the semester. But then they passed that fucking bill saying there would be a vote on whether to make people get marked, and all the guys on YouTube started talking about how the only way to be safe, long-term, was to buy your own apartment because otherwise you'd just end up on the street when the powers that be made the mark a requirement and then he panicked and applied for like a million jobs and asked Viktor if he knew of anything and then Viktor hired him down at the harbour and he was put on the same shift as Eldór. Since then a whole year had passed and he still hadn't quit and there were only six weeks until the vote and he hadn't saved enough for an apartment and he couldn't see any way he was going to and his stomach was killing him every day and the trex wasn't enough any more to calm him down.

Then he looked up and the guys in the circle were all nodding and they said they understood and he felt like if he said one more word he'd start crying in front of all of them and so he swallowed and swallowed to keep it all down and someone thanked him and asked if Eldór wanted to share his story and so Tristan stopped talking. And after the meeting Magnús Geirsson came over and offered them this gig.

The door finally opens and Magnús Geirsson appears, puffing his cheeks out like balloons. They both stand up and shake his hand.

'Hello, my boys,' says Magnús Geirsson. 'How are you feeling?'

'Good,' says Eldór.

'Me too. A little stressed, maybe,' says Tristan.

'No reason to be. We're so grateful and pleased with you boys. Hear me? This is as brave as it gets. This is exactly what people need to hear. Your side. How this nonsense is limiting your potential, your futures.' He looks from Eldór to Tristan, from Tristan to Eldór. 'Who wants to go first?'

'Me,' says Tristan.

'Good deal. It'll be about twenty minutes, Eldór,' says Magnús Geirsson, walking into the room ahead of Tristan.

'Somehow it all turns out somehow, man,' Tristan says to Eldór. Eldór laughs. Tristan follows Magnús into the studio, where two other guys are standing behind a big camera that's pointed at a black stool with a white background behind it. As he sits down, he remembers the author's name: Hafþór fucking Laxness.

5.

Vetur dreams of Daníel, that he's got into the neighbour-hood. She wakes up at four o'clock, and lies between sleep and waking until morning; she's clammy, her head pounding from fatigue. She's read everything she can find on the issue. The internet says a 'rejected' stalker is the most dangerous kind, the one most likely to follow through on threats. The one most likely to break in, do physical harm, murder. When she tries to find endings or solutions, what becomes of the vic-tims, the internet says most victims quit social media, change jobs, and ultimately, relocate. Go somewhere they can feel safe again. Most victims have PTSD like her. Most never real-ly recover. There's no happy ending. There's loss, capitulation.

The testing team is setting up in a little room on the same wing as her classroom. She hates it when other teachers or parents stick their heads in and watch her teach, but now she can't help herself, she stands outside the door and counts four people – a technician in the middle of the room busy-ing himself with the chair, a nurse over by the window, and a man and woman by a desk near the door. They're gazing at two big screens in front of them. Vetur guesses that the man is a psychiatrist and the woman a neuropsychologist. The man looks from the screen to her and for a split second, she sees herself through his eyes, this shapeless schoolmarm wrapped in a warm sweater, and she nearly sticks her tongue out at him, just to tear this image of herself to shreds, but instead, she says, 'Good morning,' and even worse, she says it in a squeaky, high-pitched voice, and then she keeps walking down the hall.

It's almost nine. The teens trickle in and sit lopsidedly in their seats; a few pull out apples and place them on their desks. Vetur looks over her class and says good morning. Then she tells them about the test, that it will be next week.

'Is this the empathy test?' asks Anna Sunna.

'Nei, nei, not at all.'

'Then what is it?' asks Tildra.

'A sensitivity assessment, just to get a general sense of where things stand. Just here at the school.'

The classroom door opens and Naómí slips in and takes her seat in theatrical silence. Myrkvi leans forward on his desk and raises his hand.

'So, uh, what do we actually have to do for this assessment?'

'You'll sit in a chair and be given a helmet to put on. Then the helmet will play all sorts of videos for you and will monitor your brain activity, the dilation of your pupils, your heartbeat and sweat production. The whole thing will take about twenty minutes.'

'That's the exact same thing I did with my psychologist last year and he said it was the empathy test,' says Anna Sunna, her palms up in a show of confusion.

'It's similar to the test, except no one has to pass,' says Vetur.

'But are they going to mark us?' asks Ylfa Sóley from the back of the class.

Vetur hesitates. Though it might be illegal to publish their results now, one never knows what will be illegal tomorrow, and, if there's anything she's learned from studying ethics, it's that more often than not, the future does not agree with the past. That's the one constant.

'No,' she says. 'No one's going to mark you.'

She's locking up when Húnbogi comes out of his classroom with an empty coffee cup.

'Hi,' he says.

'Hi.'

His wheat-blond hair is brushed back from his forehead and mussed at the back. They amble towards the teachers' lounge.

'What does the word *firring* mean? Etymologically,' she asks.

'*Firring*,' he repeats, rubbing his eyes. 'Alienation. I'm not sure. I can find out.' He looks at her. 'How are you feeling about all this?'

'Let's just say that conviction is a dwindling resource in my life.'

Húnbogi smiles broadly. Their co-workers are standing in a knot by the coffee machine, clinging to it like electrified hair. She and Húnbogi slow to a stop before they get within earshot.

'What I'm most afraid of are my own reactions,' she adds.

'How so?'

'If someone tests below the norm. What if I accidentally discriminate against them or am suddenly afraid of them without meaning to be? I can feel it when people are afraid of me. It makes me feel like there's something's wrong with me.'

'I'm a bit afraid of you, now that you mention it,' says Húnbogi.

'Don't I know it. Trembling in your boots,' she says. When he takes a sip of coffee, she notices, without meaning to, what nice forearms he has.

Suddenly, he gets embarrassed, looks down into his cup, and she can feel that it's true, that he really does tremble around her. He looks at her out of the corner of his eye and he can feel that she feels it, and they both feel it as they stand there with their coffee cups, the truth vibrating between them.

'*Jæja*,' he says.

'Já,' she says.

'Well, I'm going get ready for my next class,' he says, and she watches him go, looks at his rolled-up shirtsleeves and the tendons and veins in his arms and his combed-back hair as her heartbeat returns to normal.

She's been in love with boys like him many times before – tall, brainy-looking boys with glasses and tucked-in shirts. She's watched them from a distance, kissed them, slept with them, started seeing them, forgotten them, remembered them, regretted them, forgotten them again. At first, she found it quite comical how seriously Húnbogi took himself, with that brainy air of his. But then she started to gravitate towards the way he rose to challenges, argued the point, like she so often had herself before she'd started keeping her mouth shut rather than saying what she thought. She isn't alone in that. There are many others who have started keeping their mouths shut.

The week passes and Húnbogi is careful not to look at her, to talk to people other than her, to sit with people other than her, but sometimes she can feel his gaze on her even though he's in the middle of a conversation, and she's careful not to meet his eyes, just washes up her bowl or refills her coffee cup and then hurries off to wherever she has to hurry off to.

On Thursday, the teaching staff get a gram from the headmistress. She asks them to come in twenty minutes early the next morning, without giving any further explanation.

'Thank you for being here on such short notice,' says the headmistress on Friday morning, in the teachers' cafeteria. 'Yesterday, I received a letter from the parents' council, which met on Wednesday evening, requesting that they be given access to a special minors' registry of the students in the school. I think it's probably best that I read the letter to you.'

She holds up her watch and projects the text in front of her:

The Viðey Quarter is a new and progressive neighbourhood, built on its belief in social responsibility,
solidarity, and open dialogue. Since the Quarter
School opened four years ago, we, the parents of the
quarter, in collaboration with the good people who
teach here, have taken an active role in determining
the school's direction and shaping its values. For this,
we are truly grateful, and we hope the administration
will continue to afford us the privilege of having a say
in school policy. At a meeting of the parents' council
this past Wednesday, 19 April, we reached a consensus
about the importance of transparency and dialogue
in this new society. As such, we ask the administration to prepare a special student registry, easily
accessible to parents, so that we will be better able to
respond to the inevitable challenges that will follow
if a child does not meet the sensitivity assessment's
minimum criteria.

    With respect,

    Sara Bergdís, chair of the parents' council

The headmistress clears her throat.

'The administration met yesterday, and we've decided to
comply with this request from the parents' council. Suppress-
ing incidents of failure – or characterising them as something
to be ashamed of – would be a contradictory and damaging
message. We need to be careful and deliberate in how we talk
about things and, more especially, how we talk to a child who

tests below the norm. A great piece of advice I've heard is to talk to the child as though they have a vitamin deficiency. Nothing to be ashamed of, just something to work on.'

Vetur's desk is by a window that looks out onto the football pitch. She watches a child kicking a stone down the pavement that leads to the school. Society is essentially trying to decide whether the statistical probability that a person will commit a crime justifies an infringement on their privacy, whether it's justifiable to sound an alarm about *potential* criminals. It's impossible to answer without breaking the question into thousands of questions: how is this probability determined? What counts as a crime? What counts as an infringement on privacy? She tried to answer this last question as an ethics student. She had completed her master's thesis as part of an interdisciplinary team that included a guy around her age who was studying psychology and an older woman who was in sociology; their project had aimed to determine whether it was ethical for the media to make people's failures public. This was not, in the context of their project, a public safety issue. Rather, they were attempting to determine if 'outing' these individuals did more harm than good for their long-term recovery. They had reached no definitive conclusion.

The consequences were manifold: a large percentage of individuals who had been outed said they experienced significant or total isolation in the wake of the media reports, a large percentage said the media had hindered their recovery and had a negative impact on their mental health. Half of the survey sample had gone into treatment the same month their failure was made public; a fifth had moved out of the country; two had committed suicide.

What surprised Vetur most was that both sides, both MASC and PSYCH, leveraged the findings of her master's project. When MASC needed statistics, they pointed to the seventy per cent who said that they'd experienced isolation and when PSYCH needed statistics, they pointed to the fifty per cent who'd sought treatment. But no one was closer to forming an opinion on this – neither Vetur and her team, nor society as a whole.

But how can her co-workers, these right-minded people, not be more circumspect when an idea like this crops up? thinks Vetur. Children and teenagers are at such a sensitive, formative age – their nervous systems are still underdeveloped – how can people be willing to take such a risk when there isn't any data for these age groups? How is it that someone – with no professional training and expertise – can say, We're going to do this, and someone else will just reply, Yes, sir, with no hesitation? Vetur knows what would have happened if she'd said Stop, said Wait a second, are you sure? Everyone would have looked at her and said, Já, of course we're sure, we're sure because of This and This and This, and then she would have said, But what about the consequences, social life, self-esteem, behaviour? Rejection leads to power struggles, which lead to violence. This kind of thing has knock-on effects, kids look at unmarked people like the bad guys in cartoons, as predators, as vermin to be killed on sight.

Kids only comprehend outlines, headlines – unmarked man in his twenties, unmarked couple of foreign origin – it's hammered into them again and again that unmarked people are dangerous, that they have different values, that they thieve and lie and cheat. That they're people who harm and rape and murder. And then someone might have said: We can't afford to argue among ourselves; we have no time to lose. And, though it may be considered a sign of intelligence to be hesitant and a sign of stupidity to be certain, though current conventions praised doubt and condemned unwavering conviction, Vetur would have nevertheless reluctantly edged her way along the dock and nudged the edge of the boat with her toe to see if it was secure before stepping on board, because that's how societies work – they agree on the fundamentals but disagree about the details, or else they aren't societies.

6.

Someone's calling. Eyja has a splitting headache and a hazy recollection of Zoé trying to tell her to take out her earbuds and take off her watches as she was passing out last night.

Her mouth tastes like fermented fruit.

Þórir's on the line. It's Tuesday, almost noon. She should be at work. She clears her throat and answers like she's running.

Þórir asks if she just woke up. He's angry.

'No,' she says. 'I'm doing yoga.'

Þórir asks if she thinks he's stupid. That he can't figure out that she's the one who started this.

'Started what?'

She knows what, answers Þórir. He's about to boil over. She suppresses a smile because he'll hear it in her voice.

'Started what, Þórir? What is it now?'

Did she mean to tell him she had no part in the rumours going around, the ones saying that he's taking credit for contract negotiations that were handled by others in the company? Like he'd been bragging that he managed to land a contract with Japan when everyone knows that was Kári, and ditto that he just barely salvaged the Finland deal when everyone knows that was Fjölnir?

'Did someone say I'd been spreading that around?' she asks disbelievingly.

No, he says angrily, but he knows it was her.

'How rude can you be?' she says.

'I don't have time for such pettiness,' she says.

'You ought to make an appointment with the house psychologist, Þórir. I'm not going to take part in this kind of hysteria.'

He splutters something, but she says she has to take a call from the Netherlands and hangs up.

She calls Natalía.

She calls Inga Lára.

She thinks about calling Eldey but decides not to. Eldey's become so difficult. Always has some little dig.

Natalía says she should file a complaint. Immediately. Apply for a therapeutic assessment and psychological treatment, bring up her horrible divorce and the workplace harassment. It obviously isn't possible to pass some test when your husband's just left you to have a baby with another woman.

Inga Lára gasps and says, Jesus. Asks how she's holding up.

Says, Oh, honey, and that she can't believe it and that this just goes to show how horribly broken the system is.

'The worst part is,' says Eyja, 'that Þórir's knocked all the weapons out of my hands. I'm no longer trustworthy. It doesn't matter that he subjected me to habitual sexual harassment or took credit for my ideas. I no longer have a voice.'

Inga Lára tries to comfort her. Says she's a good person and doesn't deserve this and it isn't fair.

Which is true.

Inga Lára says she's the strongest person she knows. She promises to say as much to the papers if it comes to that. The world needs to know she's the Alpha she is. That she's a torchbearer. Someone who lets her actions speak for her.

'Yes,' she says.

'I *am* a torchbearer,' she says.

'I *do* let my actions speak for me.'

She calls Breki and Zoé says the number is not in service.

She makes a few more calls. Tests the water.

Wears her best skirt suit to the board meeting.

Observes her colleagues' body language.

She tells them about a new start-up she's received a tip about.

The company is Norwegian; they produce filter motors for ships and trawlers. The filters extract carbon dioxide from the ocean twice as fast as comparable technology on the market and use the same amount of fuel.

An enthusiastic wave washes over her colleagues. They vote and she gets the green light to start conversations.

She watches as Þórir scans the group; she says nothing.

There are two things she has to do: show the board he's not a good leader and that marking the company would be financially disadvantageous.

There are seven of them. Alli and Fjölnir are with her. They just need one more person.

That person is Kári.

After the meeting, she takes the elevator down with Kári.

'Don't worry about the thing with the Swedes,' she says. 'Happens to the best of us.'

Kári is dumbfounded. Asks why he should be worried. He had nothing to do with the Swedish company's contract.

'Oh,' she says.

'I was told it was your deal?' she says.

Kári says he's been buried in negotiations with the Japanese power plant all month.

'My misunderstanding,' she says.

Some idiot's leaning on their horn when she drives up out of the parking garage. She looks in her rear-view mirror and sees it's Fjölnir.

Fjölnir doesn't come to work the next day.

Or the day after.

Finally, she sees him outside her office.

He looks up and down the hall and whispers that Þórir fired him. He didn't pass that pity-party of a test.

That fucking ferret refuses to see reason, Fjölnir says. Þórir said he's *combing the lice from the hair of the company*.

'Shit,' she says. 'I'm sorry, man. After all the awards you've raked in for the company. That's terrible.'

Fjölnir says he's spoken to Alli. They're going to rally

support, ask the other board members whether they really think that Fjölnir is an acceptable casualty on the way to getting this bullshit stamp of approval.

He asks if he can count on her support.

'Of course,' she says.

'Let me know if I can help,' she says.

She calls a lawyer and asks about her rights.

The lawyer says that everything's been done by the book. She has a right to treatment upon the presentation of her test results – twice-weekly therapy appointments if she's so inclined. A subsidy from the pension fund if she chooses to go to a rehab centre.

The lawyer is cautious.

Speaks to her like a doctor might to an invalid.

She says thank you, sends a few messages, and gets a recommendation for another lawyer.

A typical brain has glowing red blotches in different areas. But on her scan, the blotches aren't blotches, but pinpricks. Like ants that have abandoned their hill.

Emotional Transmission, Joy: Minimum response.

Emotional Transmission, Friendship: Minimum response.

Emotional Transmission, Pain: Does not demonstrate minimum response.

Pain of Others (Same Gender): Does not demonstrate
minimum response.

Pain of Others (Different Gender): Does not demonstrate
minimum response.

Pain of Others (Same Ethnicity): Does not demonstrate
minimum response.

Pain of Others (Different Ethnicity): Does not demonstrate
minimum response.

Conclusion: Does not meet the minimum criteria.

She reads these words and knows, in spite of them, that
these are precisely her strengths, no matter what society says.

They are what gives her an edge over others.

Gylfi the Octopus invites her out to dinner on Friday.

He works at an international investment firm, too. A firm
famous for absorbing people who've lost their jobs because
of the marking.

He says *takk fyrir síðast*, thanks for last time. His smirk
like a badge of honour.

He says he hasn't been able to think of anything else all
week.

He says he heard about her and Breki a while back.

He asks what happened.

'He cheated on me with a co-worker,' she says. 'She's having a baby any time now.'

66

Nei, shit, Gylfi says. Like his football team just conceded a goal.

'You're no better,' she says.

He pulls a face and tilts his head to one side, says that things have been over between him and his wife for a long time. They've slept in separate bedrooms for years. But they stay together for the girls. The youngest is about to be confirmed in the spring and the middle one starts sixth form in the autumn.

He projects a picture of three blond girls up between them.

'Aren't they beautiful,' she says.

Yeah, he says. They are. But how is she holding up? After the divorce? Things are probably way different for her than him. He can see the divorce coming. Had things been strained between them, or did it come out of nowhere, a bolt from the blue?

She thinks for a moment.

'A bolt from the blue,' she says.

'But I'm seeing a psychologist to work through it, and everything is on the upswing. Slowly but surely.'

He says that's good to hear. He has every faith she'll kick this. There should be a law that you have to give some forewarning. Not just wham, bam, thank you, ma'am, so long, bye bye.

He looks pleased with himself every time she laughs. Presses his lips together to conceal his smile.

'I'm just happy to be free of it,' she says.

She fidgets with her napkin.

'I didn't see how small I'd become in my marriage until he left me. I have room to grow again, back to my normal size.'

She continues:

'Breki is the kind of man who says he wants a woman who challenges him. An equal.'

'But as soon as I surpassed him, he started tearing me down. He scolded me for being sure of myself. Scolded me for standing my ground. Most often, he scolded me for some tone in my voice. I started to question everything I said.'

'The minute I made a higher salary than him, he started asking for kids. He said if I didn't want kids, I had to tell him right then. If I didn't want kids, he was going to find himself another woman.'

'I told him I couldn't have kids right away, not before I became a shareholder. Then he started talking about freezing eggs. He wouldn't stop.'

'I got a promotion, frozen eggs, I got a management award, frozen eggs. Whenever I did well, it was like his eyes morphed into frozen eggs.'

Gylfi is handsome when he laughs. He doesn't hold back.

Of course he's handsome.

He wouldn't have made it to where he's made it if he didn't have dark hair and chiselled features. If he didn't have that authority in his voice.

If he didn't remind you of some animal way up the food chain. A bear. A lion.

'You're handsome when you laugh,' she says.

68

He looks at her lips. She takes a sip of wine.

The main course is served and he asks how it's going at work. How Þórir is tackling the situation.

'He sent us to be tested last week,' she says.

Gylfi's steak knife stops halfway to his plate and he looks up. Asks if she's serious. Swears. He can't believe it. Thought Þórir was made of sterner stuff than that.

Nei, shit, he adds, setting his cutlery aside, a bite of steak still on his fork. He leans back in his seat and looks out over the dining room. Has anyone been fired?

'Not that I know of,' she says.

'It just happened.'

'But I've started looking around. I don't want to deal with this.'

Gylfi looks at her for a few seconds. Then he says she should come work for them, no question.

'For you?' she repeats.

'You want me to work for you?'

He nods eagerly, his eyebrows raised.

'And what, hypothetically, would I do for you?'

He says she could keep doing what she's doing now. That's where the real money is, of course; he himself is working with catastrophe bonds, too. When people are desperate, they'll buy anything.

'Well, this is interesting,' she says.

'Já,' she says.

'I'll give it some thought.'

'First I need to find out if I passed the damn test or not.'

He says the test doesn't matter. Or, actually, yeah, if she didn't pass, that would be an excellent recommendation in itself. A stamp of quality, you might say. It would show she was cut out for real business.

She tells him about the filter motor. Says it will be a real shame if Þórir reaps the benefits. Gylfi gets a glint in his eye. When she says that certain international investors have purchased stock, he starts squirming in his seat.

They take a cab to hers. He's practically rabid on the way, keeps offering her gold and green forests. Blathers and blathers about what she could do for his firm. Where she'd start and where she could end up.

She burns all over. She wants him despite everything.

He is not a good lover.

She doesn't have a headboard she can tie him to.

The way he humped her like an old bike pump last time. His tongue like a . . . like a what?

Like a bread hook in a standing mixer.

7.

Tristan can't stop checking his bank account, just to see the balance, just to get a fucking high from seeing the balance. For the first time in a whole week, he doesn't feel completely shattered inside. He feels like Magnús Geirsson and the interview guys opened him up for all intensive purposes, unzipped him like a hoodie. He thought he was just going to say the same thing he did at the MASC meeting, that he had to move out and quit school and all that. But then they asked him about his dad and mum and brother and then Sölvi and his sister. He wasn't ready for those fucking questions, so he just told them everything, that Sölvi had given them stuff and pizza and sweets and that he was a lot more fun than their dad (he hopes his dad doesn't see this) and that Sölvi always took their side when their mum was being a pain and how she hated it, screamed that he was turning them against her, and that she could see what he was doing. He explained that his mum was always imagining stuff like that, imagining that people were always in some weird emotional war (he had NOT meant to fucking say that) and that she and Sölvi used to fight every single day and then suddenly he and Rúrik started doing all this bad shit, suddenly they were just breaking the rules, and breaking the rules was easy and they'd never been good at anything before. They weren't good at school and they weren't good at football and they weren't good at computer games because they didn't have the right computers and those three things were basically the only things you could be good at.

Then they wanted to talk more about Rúrik and he got stressed and tried to change the subject but they kept going back to his brother so he told them that Rúrik failed when he was eighteen (he definitely definitely did not mean to fucking say that) and that he'd been sent into psychotherapy and forced to take pills or else he wouldn't be allowed to live at home any more and now that he's thinking about it, Rúrik was dead-arse young at the time, he still had acne all over and couldn't grow a real beard or anything. The psychologists even said he was probably too young, that boys like Rúrik, þú veist, who were hyper and jumpy, you know, they often had to wait until they were literally twenty-five or something to be able to pass the test. But Rúrik got all these fucking pills that would supposably wake up whatever hormones, all sorts of oxy shit and then trex, and of course, Rúrik became a trextzel after a year and one guy asked what a trextzel was and Tristan explained that it's someone who's hooked on trex, you got all twisted up, þú veist, you were a pretzel for trex, or at least, that's what he thought it meant. Then he said that Rúrik had dropped out and actually quit coming home at all because he had some girlfriend or something and then one day, he got picked up with a huge bag of trex after they made it illegal and he was inside for a year, and then like a week or something after he got out he got in that fight, that stupid fucking fight about nothing, and then he got arrested for assault and now he's halfway done with his sentence.

Sæbraut–Sægarður, says the AI voice on the S. He gets off and starts walking as fast as he can towards the harbour.

They asked Tristan about the future and what opportunities he had, if he'd experienced prejudice and discrimination and all that and he told them about his race to get an apartment so he wouldn't end up living in a fucking warehouse or on the street or something worse, but he didn't actually have a clue what he wanted to do, he was never good at school, maybe he could be a carpenter or something like that, he couldn't be a plumber or an electrician or anything because you have to go into people's houses and of course everyone is marking their houses. But yeah he wanted to work somewhere not the harbour (why the FUCK had he said that? Viktor would see it) but he couldn't get a job anywhere else and there were always more and more places that unmarked people couldn't go. Like, if he wanted to buy something to eat, he had to order stuff to be sent to his apartment because shops don't trust unmarked people and some gyms don't either.

Then they asked him about buying an apartment, if he had anyone helping him, whether he had some kind of . . . safety net . . . he had to ask what they meant by safety net, was that some kind of workplace safety protocol? And then all the guys started laughing and especially Magnús Geirsson, he laughed like a fucking troll. Is there anyone who can help

73

you, money-wise, asked Magnús, and Tristan said No, and then someone said, No one? And it made him feel so goddamn sad he had to swallow twice before he said, No, no one, and the guys got all quiet and embarrassed and then thanked him for coming.

When he gets to work, Eldór has started unloading down at D1. Eldór claps him on the shoulder pretty hard, and Tristan says, Dude, but Eldór isn't listening. He's looking up at the tower where the guy from customs is sitting and scratching his fucking arse. Wojciech and Oddur are over in D2. Zoé tells him a guy on YouTube he follows has uploaded a new video and he listens to it while he starts steering the containers where they're supposed to go.

Sad news. L10N has crossed over. Just saw this morning.
I'd had my suspicions, of course, from his grams. And then
just now, he's started saying they could help me, and that
I should definitely give them a call. It is what it is. First
they say they want to help you re-enter society and learn
about yourself and get to know your own boundaries.
Then they say you should try going to therapy once. Then
twice. Then they try to get you to go on pills and tell you
you're ready to take the test and that it'll change everything.
That's how they got my best friend and now he's totally
brainwashed, he drank the Kool-Aid. He has to take the
test every year and he's stopped going to unmarked places
and stopped hanging out with unmarked people. His

74

girlfriend is marked, too, and I know she's telling him to cut me off because I'm not good enough any more or something. We've been friends since we were little kids and the one time I saw him he told me I had to take the test and go to therapy, called it a total gamechanger. It's like as soon as he got in and was accepted by this cult he forgot all the bad shit that happened. He forgets that once it was him who wasn't allowed into restaurants. He forgave the system as soon as it started working for him. Even though it exploited him and held him down before. Even though it made him feel terrible about himself.

After an hour, Viktor comes over.

'There's a container coming in from the countryside today,' he says.

'What time?' asks Eldór.

'Quarter to five,' says Viktor. 'I'll send a message when it's about an hour away and one of you go poke Fart Juice.'

They laugh. They always laugh when Viktor calls the customs guy Fart Juice. They work until noon and eat in the cafeteria. Then they go back to steering full containers onto a blue ship on its way to Denmark or Spain or somewhere around there. At four o'clock, Eldór calls the customs guy, who comes and opens random containers and checks the stuff inside. Then he goes back up to the tower to scratch his arse. The container from the countryside arrives and they stack it somewhere in the middle, among other containers that have already been checked. Tristan has done it a million times, but every time, he starts sweating like a fucking pig in his overalls and Zoé asks if he's okay because his heart is beating so fast.

At the end of the day, Viktor asks if they want a ride and they jump in, Oddur, Wojciech and Eldór.

'I'm meeting a guy right over there,' says Tristan.

'Where? I'll drop you,' says Viktor.

'Thanks, but no joke it's like literally right there. I'll see you guys tomorrow,' he says, gives them a two-fingered salute goodbye like a soldier, and walks in the opposite direction before they can say anything else. He sees the car disappear around the corner. Every time Tristan gets a ride from him, Viktor says something he doesn't want to hear. Something about some bitch he picked up downtown and fucked four times, or that they beat the shit out of some dude because the dude said something he shouldn't have said. Viktor's words feel like superglue. When Tristan was little, he was always using superglue to get revenge on Rúrik or his mum. First he superglued little rocks in their shoes and then he saw a video on the internet where some guy put superglue in his friend's hair gel and his hair got stiff and then he tried to comb his hair and his hand got glued to the comb and the comb got glued to his hair. Tristan tried to do it twice but the first time, the glue hardened before Rúrik used the gel and the second time Rúrik figured it out, just by looking at Tristan's face, and he twisted Tristan's arm behind his back so hard that Tristan started to cry and then their mum screamed at Rúrik and grounded him from going out and seeing his friends for a whole week, which ended up with Rúrik breaking the mirror in the front hall and then their mum grounded him for longer, for two weeks, no computer, and Rúrik didn't talk to Tristan the whole time. He remembered that felt like that half a month would never end. And the whole time, all he wanted was to be able to fix it.

Sometimes, Viktor asks him to fix things. Sometimes, he calls him up at night and asks Tristan to be driver and then there's nothing to do but say yes. After what happened in November, he tries not to let Viktor get too close, tries to hold him as far off as he fucking can but not too far because then Viktor would be able to feel it and try to tighten his grip. Tristan has seen it happen. Like when Wojciech said he needed time out because he'd just had a kid and his girlfriend didn't want him to be away so much at night and Viktor said, I get it, a hundred per cent, and said congratulations and then wouldn't fucking leave Wojciech alone, called him every night to order him to do something and when Eldór and Tristan said they could do it, Viktor always said, No, Wojciech was going to do it. Then one night, Wojciech came out to the car and said he couldn't come because his girlfriend was threatening to throw him out if he didn't put their daughter first and Viktor just looked at him and stared silently out the front window and Eldór and Tristan didn't say anything either and then he got in the car and Viktor drove off.

Tristan knows he'll need to be smart when he quits working at the harbour. As soon as he gets a job somewhere else,

Viktor is going squeeze him even tighter for a few weeks, just like he did with Wojciech, and then after that he'll relax again and hopefully all Tristan will have to do is drive some car back and forth and then maybe Viktor will just forget him when some new guy starts in his place. If he ever gets a fucking job, that is. These fucking companies never even give you a chance to come in for an interview. He's applied for a thousand jobs, for months, ever since he saw how fucking dangerous Viktor was back in November, which is how he ended up messing things up with Sunneva, who hasn't answered him since then, just that one time when she was drunk at some party in January.

He has half a trex when he sits down on the S-line and plays a new gram on YouTube.

'Have you noticed that when an unmarked person does something wrong everyone makes a big deal that they're unmarked, but when a marked person does something wrong, no one says anything about it? For example, the Reykjavík cops say that over the weekend, a man in his twenties was arrested for drunk driving. When a person is marked, he breaks the law because he's human, but when an unmarked person breaks the law, it's because he's unmar—'

The video stops and ad music starts playing. Tristan closes his eyes so he won't have to look at Ólafur Tandri.

'In Iceland, young men aged eighteen to twenty-five are four times more likely to commit suicide than women of the same age. Suicide is the most common cause of death among young Icelandic men. It does not have to be like this. Help is available. Let's talk about our feelings.'

The ad ends and the video he was watching starts back up. He pauses and asks Zoé to relax him and Zoé puts on piano music and shows him a picture of a green meadow with trees and a lake and stuff. She tells him to focus on his breath and inhale for four seconds and exhale for eight.

He will have enough for a down payment. He's going to get there. He closes his eyes and breathes in for four beats and out for eight but his anger increases with every breath. The fucking balls on Ólafur Tandri, to target them, the guys that HE'S killing. They won't have a chance after this vote. They won't be able to get a loan for an apartment or a job or have a normal fucking life, and then Tristan gets off the S and he's so mad he could fucking kill someone, destroy something, and there's Ólafur Tandri's house, right there in his fucking neighbourhood. Tristan is in front of the house, he walks back and forth on the pavement, and it would be so easy to ring the bell and show HIM what it's like to be fucking afraid, always, to not be able to sleep without feeling like rats are eating you from the inside out. And there he is, that fucking psychslut, with his fucking perfect blond wife, in their fucking perfect white kitchen. Tristan breathes through his nose and counts to ten like Rúrik taught him to do. He lifts his arm and takes a picture of them with his watch and then finds the spray he uses at work and makes a big X on the front door so that Óli will know that HE has also been targeted and then he walks home with his hood up and when he gets home, he writes down everything he thinks of, EVERYTHING, and with every word it's like he feels a little bit better and he keeps going until he doesn't have any more words in him.

8.

On Tuesday, Óli receives another death threat. Or new treatise, more like: the letter-writer describes, in great detail, how he plans to snip off Óli's eyelids and slit his family's throats. Accompanying the message is a photo of him and Sólveig from the night before, taken through the kitchen window. They have their backs turned to one another, absorbed in their tasks, or perhaps their unhappiness. Probably both. He speaks to a policewoman who tells him they'll check the footage.

Óli looks out the window and sees Himnar parked out front. When Óli gets in the car, Himnar is watching something in private mode; when he leans over his friend's shoulder, all Óli can see are pink and yellow refractions. Himnar shuts off the projection, says hi, but then is suddenly transfixed by something behind Óli. Óli follows his gaze. Someone has sprayed a big, red X on their front door.

'I've been marked,' says Óli.

'Bastards,' says Himnar.

He turns off the engine and they both go to the door. Himnar puts a thumb on the colour and rubs.

'Já, já. It'll come off,' he says and shows Óli his thumb.

'Maybe Sólveig didn't see it,' says Óli. 'Maybe she just went straight out.'

Himnar gives him a sympathetic frown.

Óli takes a picture of the door and calls the policewoman back to report the vandalism. While they're talking, he runs up and gets a rag and sponge and fills a bucket with hot water. When he's done, he goes back down and hands Himnar the rag.

'Nah, I want the sponge.'

'C'mon, Himnar,' says Óli in annoyance.

'What?' says Himnar, laughing. Óli hands him the sponge and sets to work on the door.

It takes them ten minutes to clean off the paint. When they finally make it into the office, his colleagues are all caught up in the projects of the day. Two people have been charged with the murder of the policeman. An MP has changed her opinion since yesterday, from opposed to in favour. Support is still hovering around sixty-five per cent. Everything's inching in the right direction. Around five o'clock, he sends Sólveig a gram saying he won't be home for dinner. She doesn't answer. He checks every few minutes to see if she's answered and every time gets a bit gloomier. If she saw the X, it only makes sense for him to mention it. But maybe she didn't see it and it's completely unnecessary to fan the flames of their discontent.

He can't focus.

'I don't know if you saw it this morning,' he writes. 'But someone sprayed an X on our front door. Himnar and I cleaned it off right away. I've called the police. Sorry I didn't say something earlier. I needed some time to process it myself. And I'm also sorry I'm so seldom home for dinner. We're so close to this being over with. There's only a month left. I love you.'

Ten minutes go by.

'Shall I pick something up on the way home?' he writes.

'Something sweet? A snack?' he adds.

No response. He tries to work. He gives up texting, starts feeling hurt by her silence. Then he gets sulky. He didn't choose this. How was he supposed to know he'd be subjected to threats and mockery? He waits another few minutes for a response. All of a sudden, he has the feeling that Sólveig is at home, preparing herself for the divorce talk. He turns around and asks Himnar if he's leaving any time soon. Himnar shakes his head without looking away from his screen. Óli calls a cab and fetches his jacket from the coat rail. When the car arrives, he asks the driver to drop him at the neighbourhood shop.

He knows what he has to do. He has to quit the campaign. Wherever their conversations begin, they always end in an argument about the mark, like tributaries flowing inexorably into the same powerful river. Over and over Sólveig repeats that a centralised psychiatric system is not the solution. That empathy is a more complex phenomenon than they're making it out to be, that criminals can be full of empathy and psychopaths entirely harmless. And although it might be possible to draw some conclusions from the frequency and correlation of these things, the shame and misfortune that accompanies failure outweighs any help that is provided.

It doesn't matter what counterarguments Óli trots out. Of course, he knows that there's no cure-all, that compulsory marking won't solve all their problems or preclude crimes and violence. Of course, he knows this isn't black-and-white. But Sólveig can't overlook these indisputable statistical facts: a) crime rates plummet in marked neighbourhoods, b) nine out of every ten people who were sentenced for a crime in the past year were unmarked, and c) one out of every four incarcerated people fails the test. But let's say that society could catch these individuals – a fourth of all those who are currently serving out sentences – and provide them with appropriate resources *before* they offend. The mark isn't a punishment, it's a preventative measure. But Sólveig thinks this is a childish way of thinking that doesn't stand up to further scrutiny, and so they continue, ad infinitum. He tries to put himself in her shoes, says he understands where she's coming from. She's an empathetic person and it's in the nature of empathetic people to see the humanity in others. But she has to understand that the psychopathic percentage takes advantage of precisely that: her compassion.

Recently, Sólveig has started closing her eyes, inhaling deeply, and telling him to stop talking to her. She does this often – when he's talking about normal stuff, too. If he makes an innocent comment, about clutter around the house, about Himnar or his father, or the neighbour who never closes the gate in the back garden so that it swings back and forth and makes a thunking sound all night, she says, 'Oh, Óli.'

Oh, Óli, like he's some absurd old man. Something

collapses inside him when she does this. He sees his father before him, sitting at the kitchen table, debating his mother to death. He sees his mother, tidying up the kitchen so she won't have to look at his father. But he's not like his father. He doesn't raise his voice. He doesn't interrupt Sólveig. He's trained himself to be soft-spoken. He's trained himself to be polite and unflappable and to listen to her side. *When you talk like this, we feel like this.*

She's trying to set boundaries for him, but she crosses those boundaries herself all the time. These reactions are clearly rooted in the mark, a seed planted so deep in their relationship that they can't uproot it.

Most recently, she asked him to stop discussing politics entirely. She wasn't going to change her opinion; this was starting to have a serious impact on their family. They'd stopped having sex and stopped spending time together. And in an attempt to defuse their arguments, Dagný had started acting like a clown when they were all together.

'She's three years old, Óli, and she's already started taking on this emotional drudgery,' she said. '*Three years old.* And I can't abide it any longer.'

'This isn't a compromise,' replied Óli.

'Nothing I do is a compromise,' she answered, throwing up her hands. 'You use psychology as extortion in our relationship.'

He feels exposed in the shop. People look at him and then quickly look away. A smartly dressed woman thanks him for the much-needed work he's doing at the same moment a slovenly woman thrusts out her chin. As he waits for his receipt at the register, a short man with greasy hair and five o'clock shadow catches sight of him.

'Hey, aren't you that shrink?'

'Yes.' Óli is calm, but instinctively tenses.

'You and your PC police are really something, you know that?' says the man, stepping towards Óli with outstretched fingers.

Someone in the shop tells the man to leave Óli alone.

Óli is about to hurry past when the man makes a grab at him.

'Nine nine nine,' says Óli, and ear-splitting sirens shriek through the shop. Everyone freezes. The man flees the scene; someone yells at him as he runs out. The police call and ask if Óli needs assistance, but he says no.

He walks home quickly.

Sólveig's face betrays nothing when he falls through the door with his shopping bags, but she does let him kiss her on the mouth.

'This is a surprise,' she says as he unpacks the bags.

'I miss you two,' he says.

He makes mushroom bourguignon with potatoes. Sólveig doesn't mention the red X. He purées a scoopful of mushrooms and uses it as a sauce with fried veggie balls for Dagný. At first, Sólveig turns down a glass of wine, but halfway through the meal she changes her mind. After dinner, they tuck Dagný in together and Sólveig sits silently at the end of the bed while he reads to their daughter. Once Dagný is asleep, they sit in the living room. He asks Zoé to play music from their university days and they're suddenly reminiscing about the past and laughing. They open another bottle of red. He keeps an eye on the sharp lines around her mouth as she speaks.

'Did you notice the door this morning?' he asks.

She looks into her glass, twirls the stem between her fingers.

'Yes.'

'I'm sorry.'

She says nothing.

'When you didn't answer today, I was sure you were getting ready to leave me,' he says.

Her mouth twists.

'I considered it.'

'Leaving?'

'Yes.'

'Sólveig,' he says. 'I'm going to quit PSYCH after the vote. I want to fix this.'

She finally looks at him and they gaze at each other for a few moments.

'You've been saying you're going to quit for a long time,' she says. He gazes at her slender neck as she sips her wine.

'I've made up my mind. I'm going to resign after the referendum, no matter what the outcome.'

'Why don't you resign tomorrow?'

'Salóme won't be able to handle it tomorrow. But she will be after the referendum. She suspects it's coming. She often says I'm headed towards a burnout.'

Sólveig doesn't say anything. She finishes her wine, stands up, and goes to bed. When he comes into the bedroom, she's under the duvet and, as usual, turns away from him. But once he's lying down, she rolls over and finds him in the darkness, for the first time in many weeks, maybe months.

Óli tries to leave work at a decent hour over the coming days. He explains the situation to his colleagues, and they understand. He gets a message from the policewoman in the middle of a news interview on Friday. He only sees part of it, but it's enough that he loses his train of thought, stares blankly at the reporter, and she has to repeat his own words back to him in order to get him on track again.

After the interview, he calls the policewoman, who says they've looked at all the footage they have from both evenings. In all likelihood, they're dealing with the same individual: on both occasions, a hooded man was spotted standing outside the house. Based on his general appearance and bearing, he's between twenty and forty; the first time, he walks straight up to the tyres, but the second time, it seems he's about to knock on the door, then hesitates and changes his mind. He can be seen taking a photo and spraying the door. After he finishes, they're able to track his progress down the street towards one of the apartment buildings on Kirkjusandur. One of those buildings that was built with singles in mind – studios on top of studios. There are almost thirty men in the right age range who have registered their legal domiciles in the building. There's no way they'll get warrants to investigate them all.

'What do you suggest we do?' asks Óli. 'The man's clearly unbalanced.'

'Is there somewhere you can move temporarily, just until after the referendum?' asks the policewoman. 'Perhaps to a family member's or friend's place?'

'Possibly,' says Óli.

But when he gets home, he doesn't say anything to Sólveig. He knows any talk of moving will strike yet another blow to their relationship. He puts off mentioning it for a day. Then he puts it off for another. Then he decides that in all likelihood, the man poses no real danger and that it would be selfish to frighten his wife and daughter any more than necessary.

9.

On Monday, the headmistress sends an announcement to parents saying the school will be preparing its own registry. Vetur expected that there would be uncertainty, questions or grams, but nothing of that sort has made its way into her mailbox. Midweek during her open-office hours, a woman peeks around her classroom door. The woman has bleached blond hair with stringy ends that brush her shoulders and Vetur knows immediately that this is a parent who wants to discuss the test.

'Hi, sorry,' says the woman. 'I'm Naómí's mum. Am I disturbing you?'

'Not at all,' says Vetur, closing the hologram in front of her and gesturing for the woman to take a seat. She says thank you and sits; she looks tired in her oversized clothes, she's somewhere around fifty and her hair is swept back from her forehead like licked icing. She introduces herself as Alexandria.

'Maybe you've heard about me from Naómí's father?'

'No, sorry? I can't say I have.'

'He's big on telling people what an unfit mother I am,' she says, and looks out at the schoolyard. 'I thought maybe he'd talked to you too.'

'I've just started,' says Vetur.

'Yeah, I know. When we moved here, he called the head-mistress and pretended he was worried about our daughter's welfare, said I couldn't take care of her. The headmistress invited us both to a meeting, which, of course, the father of my child did not show up for. He made up some excuse at the last minute. Which gave me the chance to tell her the truth.'

Vetur tries to form a question mark with her face: she fur-rows her brow, tilts her head.

'He can't get into the neighbourhood,' says Alexandria. 'He isn't marked.'

'I see,' says Vetur.

'We moved last summer. Naómí started here in Septem-ber, like you,' she says. 'Anyway, I haven't been able to sleep for two nights in a row, after I saw the thing about the school registry. I moved to this neighbourhood because we had to get away from Naómí's father and I thought we'd be safe here. We almost never have to go outside the double gates. Everything's here. Naómí takes her dance classes in the neighbourhood with her friends and if they want to go to the movies or into town, I give them a ride. But now I'm lying awake at night and wondering what will happen after Naómí takes the test.'

Alexandria hangs her head, swallows.

'She's so difficult,' she whispers. 'I can't keep her in check. What if she fails and all the other parents see it, what hap-pens then? What if her new friends dump her, and what if the rules of the neighbourhood change? They could lower the test-taking age from eighteen to sixteen or fourteen. And what if her dad finds out? He might be able to use it to start a new custody battle.'

She sniffs deeply, once, twice, and then she starts to sob. Vetur hurries over to her and puts an arm around the woman's swollen shoulders.

'May I ask, do you have a good psychologist? Have the two of you gone together?'

'I don't see a psychologist any more,' says Alexandria, her voice shriller than before, as if there's an air bubble trapped in her windpipe. She clears her throat. 'I went to a woman named Gréta for a long time, but I couldn't keep seeing her.'

Alexandria dries her eyes with the arm of her sweater and tries to regain control of her voice.

'She started talking down to me, it was horrible. Over and over again, like an older sister or an old friend who knows you so well they don't respect normal boundaries any more. She would scold me sometimes like I was this little kid. In the end, I said, You know what? I'm not going to let myself be treated like this any more. But ever since I quit seeing her a year ago, I feel people judging me whenever they find out, I feel their whole attitude change. Like I must be a mess because I'm not working on my inner life or something. It's like everything's been turned upside down.'

'But then how do you work through things?'

Alexandria sighs in another attempt to still her tears and her lower lip trembles. 'I talk to friends sometimes. When they feel like taking my calls. They all work, of course, and can't spend their time blabbing on the phone like me. But yeah, I know, I need to do something about my issues. I get it, a hundred per cent.'

'Does Naómí have a good psychologist?'

'Oh yes, she sure does. Everything that happens between us, every conversation we have, she tells her psychologist, and they twist it around and then she comes home and screams at me that Silla said this, and Silla said that, and that I'm fat and stupid and should never have been allowed to raise children.'

A drop of saliva sprays out of her mouth with the last word and lands on the desk. They both look at it.

'I'm sorry I'm dumping on you like this,' says Alexandria, with a regretful frown. 'It's just, I can't sleep any more. I lie there for hours, stuck between sleeping and waking, imagining what might happen.'

'It'll be fine,' says Vetur, standing up and moving back to the other side of the desk. 'If Naómí doesn't pass, unlikely as that is, then it's better we know now than when she turns eighteen. When under great stress, the brain's normal reaction is to protect itself by putting up emotional defences. Nothing to be ashamed of.'

'That's not true,' says Alexandria. Vetur is shocked at the sudden sharpness of her voice. 'Sorry, but I just can't stand when people say that. "It's nothing to be ashamed of." It's like an empty milk carton in the fridge. You think you have enough in there, but then you reach for it, and you've got nothing.'

She sees something in Vetur's expression that pulls her up short.

'I'm sorry,' she says. 'That's obviously not your fault. It's just something you hear people say a lot.'

Alexandria wrings her hands.

'I failed it myself, two years ago. There was a lot going on.'

'I see,' says Vetur, feeling the woman's contours take on new shapes – her stringy hair, swollen limbs and lack of psychologist. An involuntary thought: she has to get rid of this woman. Get her out of the room. Vetur tries to shut off the thought, expel it. Alexandria says something and Vetur tries to listen, but a wave of terror is breaking over her, flowing towards her, and then it happens: Daníel enters the room, hands in the pockets of his jeans. He looks at her, capable of anything. The classroom turns to jelly.

'Are you okay?' she hears Alexandria say.

'Yes,' she hears herself reply. She white-knuckles the desk in front of her.

She focuses on a knot in the light-coloured wood, gives herself as long as she needs to reground herself. Waits for him to leave the room. When she looks up, she's not sure if it's been a few seconds or a few minutes. Alexandria is sitting on the other side of the desk, alert, concerned.

'I apologise,' she says. 'Just felt nauseous for a moment.'

'Ugh, sorry,' says Alexandria with a grimace.

'I recommend that Naómí take the assessment,' says Vetur. 'If you elect not to send her, it will look much worse than if she fails. If she doesn't achieve the minimum criteria, we'll ask for a meeting with the headmistress and decide on the next step together.'

Vetur stands up to indicate that the meeting is over; this catches Alexandria unawares for a moment, but then she stands up as well.

'Thanks for coming in,' says Vetur.

'Yeah,' says Alexandria. 'Thank you.'

As soon as she's left the room, Vetur locks the door, goes over to the window and looks out to the car park, even though she knows that Daníel isn't there, that's impossible.

The medication makes her feel funny. Freer somehow. Her psychologist is sitting across from her, and inside the helmet she's wearing there appears a violet dot that goes back and forth on a horizontal line and then up and down a vertical one. Vetur follows it with her eyes.

'Where are you stuck?'

'It's two weeks after Daníel broke into my apartment. I'm back home after staying with Mum and Dad for a week. I'm washing up after dinner when I see the black Benz. It's parked on the other side of this big field that's behind the apartment building. I can just make out Daníel's outline in the driver's seat. I freeze. I don't know how long he's been watching me. A few hours? A few days? The sense of security I've cobbled together since the restraining order went into effect crumbles in an instant. He's been careful to stay more than fifty metres away from me so that Spotter won't report him. I take a picture of the car and send it to the cops, who arrive shortly after and make Daníel leave. I'm told he's been given a warning. I ask the cops if it's possible to increase the distance from fifty metres to two hundred, but they say that to do that, I'd have to press charges again.

'That same evening, I get my first panic attack. I go to the ER and tell the woman at reception I'm having a heart attack. I'm given a tranquilliser; I go back to Mum and Dad's and ask my neighbour to go in my apartment periodically to turn different lights on and off in the hope of misleading Daniel. Three days later, the black Benz is parked up the street from and diagonal to my parents' house, half-hidden behind some hedges. Dad storms out to confront Daniel, but as soon as he gets close, the car drives away. The cops record the incident and tell us that Daniel has been added to a list of repeat offenders and will be fined. The third time, a few days later, I'm shopping with Mum; we're in the car park when I see him. He's closer than before. I can make out the outline of his face. Mum asks what's wrong; the Benz starts up, then disappears around the corner.'

She focuses on the violet dot moving along the horizontal axis in the helmet.

'I'm learning to recognise panic attacks. I know that when I start to feel pins and needles up and down my limbs, it won't be long before I start to hyperventilate. I can't sleep normally any more. I wake twenty, thirty times a night and always feel like he's standing over me. Then I get my results: I've passed the test and can mark myself if I want to. The school doesn't require it, it's enough for them to know I've passed. Up to that point, I've been sceptical about the mark. But in that moment, I don't think twice, I add my name to

97

the Registry and hope with my whole being that Daníel will fail so that maybe he'll seek help. I check every hour to see if his status has changed from unmarked to marked.

'When the school admin tells me Daníel has resigned due to illness, relief floods through me. He must have failed, I think to myself, and that means there are places in this city where I'm safe, where he can't get in. Not long after, I see him for the fourth time, outside my mum and dad's house again. That's when I press charges. I tell the police that he resigned due to illness right after the school staff was tested and my legal advocate's manner changes immediately. The district court issues another restraining order the next day. He's not allowed to come near me for the next twelve months, the fifty metres is extended to two hundred, and I'm told that he's agreed to rehabilitation and psychological treatment.'

'That's great,' says her therapist, peering at Vetur's brain activity, which is projected in front of her. 'Your short-term memory only illuminated at the beginning. Almost everything has moved over to your long-term memory. We're getting somewhere.'

Most people's field of vision is two hundred and ten degrees. Every opinion, every single little stance you take, depends on where you're positioned, who you're talking to, what you've seen. When it comes down to it, an opinion is nothing but a decision about where you're going to look and what you're going to turn your back on. It's probable that Vetur was more tolerant before she met a man with a moral disorder who failed the test, probable that she wouldn't have thought there was anything particularly notable about Naómí's adolescent attitude a year ago, but now she has to force herself not to read too much into the girl's facial expressions, which now seem more selfish than they used to, uglier, more dangerous than before; she has to force herself not to psychoanalyse the fact that Naómí comes to class with an apple every single day – without fail – and that she's as loud as she is and as trend-obsessed, that her every movement is a performance, her every word dramatised.

That night, she goes to her parents' house for dinner. After lying on the sofa for a long time, half chatting, half watching a crime drama, she waits for her dad to drive her home, where she lies in bed, fully clothed on top of the duvet, trying to prepare herself to meet the coming day, to soothe her anxiety, to embrace her scrawny students, to be strong for these know-nothings who think they know everything and yet ask Where is Mexico? and Where is Akureyri?, all of them still gaping beaks in the nest, always hungering for something – entertainment, recognition, independence – picking their noses, tearing down the hallways in games of tag, yanking on their willies.

It's not a question of conviction, she says to herself the next day, when a Year Eight boy puts his head down on his desk, his shoulders shaking with sobs. It's a question of achieving the greatest good for the greatest number, she says to herself later when the first rumours start circulating about two failures, both in Year Twelve. She tries as best she can to remain impassive when her class arrives in tense, unusual silence for their Emotional Skills lesson, acting as though the issue of testing wasn't of any great concern.

'Yes?'

'What does dehumanise mean?'

'Dehumanise?'

'Yes.'

'Why do you ask?'

'I heard my dad say it yesterday.'

Vetur thinks for a moment.

'It's when you think another person is so different from you that you don't feel compassion for them any more.'

The school week ends – finally – and Yes, she's definitely up for going to 104.5 and Yes, thank you, she will take the sofa instead of a chair, and when she flops onto the sofa with her glass of red wine, she can feel the stress leaving her body, seeping from her lower back and out into her hips.

'I figured out where the word *firring* is derived from,' says Húnbogi, sitting next to her. 'In Old Norse, *firr* means further, *firri* means even further still, and *firrast* is the reflexive verb, to keep away, to shun, to avoid. Which is how we get to the modern-day form, *firring*, or alienation. There you have it.'

'There I have it.'

They both act like nothing special has occurred, like they don't both know that he's made a concerted effort not to talk to her at all since last week, probably because he'd accidentally showed his hand, and he's also probably not sure if his crush is mutual, or if he's just being inappropriate and pushy at work, and actually, she isn't sure herself if she has a crush on him or if she's just seeking the same old high she gets from the admiration. At least she's aware of it now, she's trying to do better.

He tells her how his class handled the test and Vetur is too tired to feel nervous around him, drinks two glasses of red wine too fast and decides not long after to go home, thinking she sees disappointment in his smile when she says goodbye to everyone without warning.

She wakes up the next day with her belongings dumped on her bed and her make-up still on. She turns off the lamp and lies there for a long time in the dark, thanks to her black-out curtains. Would she have passed the test when she was fourteen? Extremely unlikely. She stole sweets and lied, was always making a fuss, was a real drama queen, constantly disrespecting other people's boundaries, and it wasn't until decades later that she began to recall such incidents and see herself clearly and feel ashamed.

A year ago, when the last school she worked at mandated that all employees take the test, she lay in this same bed for days, worried she'd fail. She lay in bed like a car stuck in the mud and spun her mental wheels. Sure, she cried over the pain of others and suffered when she saw other people suffering, but she was no angel – she was an expert when it came to scamming the bus system and had lied to her professors to get deadline extensions, she'd give herself a bigger slice of cake if she could get away with it (something she still does), and she'd cheated on her boyfriend when she was twenty-one years old, with a boy who'd once rejected her (the worst thing she'd ever done). Being empathetic didn't make her a saint. In her heart, she knew she didn't feel for just anyone. Whether she let the pain of others affect her depended on what information she had, on the circumstances, on how things were going in her own life. And this self-knowledge is why she agreed with the critiques levelled by ethicists who said that, while empathy could be a great indicator as to whether a person is likely to do harm to someone else, it was far from being a perfect metric.

She closes her eyes and tries to relax her body.

We almost never have to go outside the double gates.

She and Alexandria are both fleeing, seeking shelter. They're both locking themselves in. She turns onto her side and sees before her the tranquil amazement on Daníel's face, half-buried in the pillow, the day after they slept together for the first time. She hides her face in the bed and is ashamed of her ego yet again, ashamed of having been so needy of recognition, for not having known better.

Tea,

Thank you so much for explaining avian migration patterns to me yet again. I've been listening to your explanations since we were twenty years old. But I'm forty now and I can no longer abide the way you speak to me, like I'm a child. It's not your job to educate me or bring me up. Like always, you've come up with your own version of how this conversation occurred: I'm the one with the outbursts, the one who called you 'a wolf in sheep's clothing' and backed you against a wall. I alone am responsible for the fact that our conversations depart the realm of 'philosophical speculation' because I'm driven by blind political correctness and trench warfare.

You act like our topic of conversation is the reason we fought, like I wouldn't endure your opposing arguments and that's why everything's turned to 'shock and awe, fire and ash', but you all too conveniently forget to account for how those opposing arguments were framed. It makes a difference, Tea. It affects the way situations progress. You spoke down to me and belittled my perspective. You laughed when I talked about the new argumentation conventions, about asking questions and listening.

But would you like to know why I mentioned these new conventions? Because for years, you haven't asked me even the slightest thing. You come over for coffee and go on and on about yourself and your problems and your triumphs and I always have to tell you, unasked, about what's going on in my life. Always. I've found this hurtful for many years, and I've taken this lack of questions as total lack of interest on your part. But after our conversation about the way they're teaching people to argue now, I finally understood that this is what you actually think a conversation is. Statements. That you say something about your life, and I say something about mine, and thus the conversation moves forward – with statements. But here's the problem with that: it's hard for me to talk about myself without being asked. It makes me feel like I'm taking up too much space and am being egocentric. Why haven't I mentioned this before? Because it's hard, Tea. This isn't something you want to ask a friend to do – to be interested in you. To ask you about your life. So instead, I mentioned this new mode of argumentation, as a way to bring it up indirectly – in the hope you'd see yourself reflected in the universal, in the philosophy behind it. Which you didn't, of course. You just laughed, like you always do when you want to make the other person feel insecure about their opinion.

I've often pitied you for this, Tea. I've often pitied you for missing out on other people's perspectives whenever you get so fixated on being right. Imagine how much you'd grow if you simply started to ask and listen and consider. If you held back just a little and thought about why it might be that people don't use the term 'psychopath' any more, but rather 'people with moral disorders'. Why Icelanders stopped using the word *siðblindingi*, or literally, a person blind to morality. Because this isn't blindness. Blindness implies that the person can't be helped, that they're incurable. But moral disorders *are* treatable. And that's aside from the obvious point that we should do away with all these caustic, one-word identifiers for good: psychopath, dyke, ginger, fatty. These words are not only offensive, they reduce a person to a single characteristic. When in reality, people are fragmented, with a million different traits, not just one. No one is just a sexuality or a skin colour or a disease.

Anyway. I've asked you a number of times not to speak down to me. But that doesn't seem to mean anything to you. So now I'm going to try something new: speak to me as if I were you. Speak to me like you'd speak to yourself.

This is the only solution if we're going to be friends for another twenty years.

Laíla

10.

Þórir calls the next day. Raving like a lunatic.

Asks how Eyja could let herself be so stupid.

Asks if her stupidity knows no bounds.

'What are you talking about, Þórir?' she asks.

If she thinks she can send him threats, he says, night after night, without consequences, she's going to be sorely disappointed.

'What are you talking about, Þórir?'

The grams, he says. The grams she sends him every night. Yesterday, she threatened to take the Norwegian start-up company with her if she left. The filter motors.

'You know what, Þórir? I don't have time for this any more.'

'Before, I would have let you call me on a Sunday and accuse me of whatever,' she says.

'But this is where I draw the line,' she says.

'There was precisely nothing in that gram that could even possibly be construed as a threat. I was just letting you know that the contract negotiations with EcoZea are going well.'

He repeats what Eyja said in the gram. Like he's reading it from a piece of paper.

He says she can work from home for the next few weeks.

He hasn't the slightest interest in seeing her face.

She makes an appointment with a maid service; an hour later, a woman arrives and does the cleaning. Meanwhile, Eyja nests in her office, looks up her favourite organic market, and puts in an order:

3 smoothies every day, 7.30 a.m.

1 dinner and 1 bottle of red wine, 7.30 p.m.

Inga Lára says she should go with Fjölnir to meet the board.

Natalía says she should wait a bit, that maybe the situation will resolve itself. That there's no reason to expose herself just yet. By law, Þórir can't say anything.

'But if this goddamn referendum is passed,' says Eyja, 'it'll be a death sentence for me regardless.'

Natalía says there's no risk of the referendum passing. The pro-mandaters are in free-fall. And even if the marking mandate does go through, it will by no means be a 'death sentence' for her.

They run through all the firm's employees. Speculate on who else might have failed.

Out of nowhere, Inga Lára says they should quit bad-mouthing. That she feels uncomfortable.

'Bad-mouthing? Who's bad-mouthing?' says Eyja.

'We're disparaging our colleagues and criticising people's work ethic.'

Two seconds' pause, and then they burst into laughter.

—

She sees on the work portal that Kári is going to work from home this week due to illness.

'Hi, I called as soon as I could. Did he fire you, that bastard?'

What? says Kári, and No, and What's going on?

'Oh,' she says. 'I thought maybe . . .'

'Well, Þórir said something about the contract with Japan and then I saw that you were working from home and got worried.'

Kári asks what Þórir said about the contract.

'Nothing concrete. It was just the context and his tone. He said whatever about the contract and then something to the effect that now that he has everyone's test results, he can finally start "combing the lice from the hair of the company".'

Kári is silent.

But he passed the test. He got his results shortly after they spoke last week.

He says he's actually home sick.

'Oh, shit, okay,' says Eyja. 'That's a relief.'

Gylfi comes over around noon and paws her like a giant puppy.

He tries to talk and undress her at the same time. Unzips her pants and tugs her shirt over her head while saying that she's got to come over and convince the Dutch company to sell the shares to them instead. He's made several phone calls. They'll outbid Þórir. She'll make such a lavish commission that she'll be able to buy shares herself if she wants.

He pulls out his purple-brown cock and lifts her onto the kitchen island; he's going to try it standing, but the counter is too high.

He attempts to carry her into the living room but drops her.

When they make it to the sofa, he gets all worked up again and pries open her mouth and shoves his tongue into it. She leans her head back and holds him off with her knees.

This excites him even more and he attempts to ease her knees apart with his hips until she finally lets him in. The moment he starts, she clamps her thighs together and he thrashes, trying to wedge his way further in. She only has to hold and release, forbid and allow twice, before he lets out a frightful sound, like he's drowning in his own larynx.

When he's gone, she distractedly projects the day's headlines for herself.

The first thing she sees is a large headshot of someone she recognises.

For a moment, she feels like she's looking at a picture of herself. It's a face she knows well. She gets her bearings: it's Fjölnir.

The photo is superimposed over another photo of their firm's headquarters.

Unexplained Firing.

Þórir leaked this.

Fjölnir must have lost his temper. Dug in his heels.

She tries calling him, but his number is out of service. She sends a gram.

She calls Kári, who says that Fjölnir and Alli spoke with Þórir on Friday and laid their cards on the table. Alli said he'd leave, too, if Fjölnir was fired. They tallied up the clients they'd brought to the company.

Clients they'd take with them if it came down to it.

And then Þórir said he'd already discussed the matter with all of the relevant parties.

The clients were aware of the changes being made within the firm. They knew the firm wanted to be on the right side of history.

She drinks smoothie after smoothie, paces back and forth.

Fucking Þórir.

Goddamn it.

Fuck.

Goddamn it.

How quick all these monkeys jump on the wagon.

The things people let themselves say.

they should all be sterlized sp they wont brEed

Former classmates say Fjölnir has always been like this.

Current colleagues who *choose to remain anonymous* say Fjölnir is still like this.

She googles everything that could potentially happen to her because of this fucking test.

Medication.

Talking therapy.

She buys an app that will prevent her calls from being traced and will disguise her voice and then rings the first name that comes up when she asks Zoé for a psychologist.

She says she's calling for her sister. Who failed the test. She asks if her sister can skip therapy and just go on meds.

The psychologist says it's not advisable.

He says the medication helps, but it also takes hard work. Her sister needs to be prepared to put in considerable effort if she wants to lead a good and normal life.

'A normal life?' she repeats. 'Who says she hasn't led a normal life? I'm positive my sister has led twice as normal a life as all the marked people in this country combined and you with them.'

The psychologist says nothing.

'That's really helpful. Thank you so much,' she says.

'Have a good day,' she says, and then hangs up.

She makes three phone calls and an hour later, a young man shows up outside her building with twenty pills.

When she gets back up to her apartment, she looks at the label on the bottle.

Oxym.

She washes one down with some red wine that evening.

She sends Breki a gram and asks him to unblock her.

Then she creates a burner account.

He's uploaded one photo since he blocked her.

A baby-bump pic of that fucking cow.

Who has that expression on her face, that soppy expression. *Aren't I lovely?* it says.

She pours herself more wine and clicks on the cow's profile.

All of a sudden, she's picturing the office where Breki and the cow work, the brightly lit cafeteria.

The cow is struggling with the coffee machine, Breki needs to use the sink.

He touches her by accident.

A spark ignites.

She feels funny.

Feels like . . . hmm, she doesn't know what.

She gets into her car without knowing where she's going.

Drives past the Viðey Quarter. Past the harbour.

Drives until she gets to the office.

In the elevator on the way up, she looks at herself and starts to smile.

Then laugh.

She's so breezy!

Everything's so breezy!

Þórir's office is unlocked.

She runs a hand over his desk. His furniture.

Weird!

She feels like . . . the top layer of her skin has been peeled off.

She hugs herself and feels a deep, deep sense of well-being.

She sees the gold-plated pen cup that she threw at Þórir's face.

The day he fired her. Já.

Pens.

Þórir loves his pens. He buys them online. One-hundred-, two-hundred-year-old pens. She reaches for one and touches her lips to it.

Sniffs.

Iron and ink.

She lets herself float from room to room.

Then she sees Kári's office at the end of the hall. Everything shipshape. He's an orderly fellow.

Oops!

She drops Þórir's pen on the floor. Nudges it with her toe.

Considers it.

It's just peeping out from under the desk now.

Like a worm in the rain.

11.

'I can't believe you still haven't done anything about this,' says his father, looking at the car in the driveway.

'It only happened two weeks ago.'

'And you'd have let it sit until Christmas, knowing you.'

His father hoists the first tyre off the bed of his truck and Óli rolls it over to his car.

'What kind of person slashes the tyres on someone's car?'

'Someone with interests to protect, I'd imagine.'

'I mean, we all have "interests to protect", but c'mon.'

His father shakes his head and once they've got all the tyres down, he finds the jack and wheel brace in the boot and holds the latter out to Óli.

'I'm not going to do it for you.'

Óli starts loosening the nuts one by one. His father leans on the car and watches.

'Did you see the latest numbers this morning?' he asks. 'Fifty-six per cent in favour. What's that? A six per cent drop in support in one week?'

'MASC paid for that survey,' says Óli, putting all his weight on the wheel brace. 'It doesn't mean anything.'

'It doesn't make any difference who pays if the sample is random,' says his father. 'It's never going to pass. There's no chance. People say they're going to vote for this foolishness now, but as soon as they're in the voting booth, they won't dare. It's way too radical.'

Óli moves to the next tyre.

'I mean, is there anything that indicates that this so-called test actually works?' his father continues. 'Couldn't these psychos just flip the switch on their empathy whenever they feel like?'

'We don't use words like "psycho" any more.'

'Oh, please, don't start with that again,' says his father, scowling. 'Until you and your cronies strike down freedom of speech, I'm going to keep calling a psycho a psycho, a fag a fag, and a looney bin a looney bin.'

Óli doesn't say anything, starts to loosen the tyres on the other side. His father has never called anyone a fag in his life. It's just a word he uses to shock people, which he learned from his own father, who also said that word to shock people.

'Anyway,' his father continues, 'one of Russia's leading experts, an internationally recognised psychologist, published an article this weekend, did you see it?'

'No.'

'He says the test is seriously flawed in that it only tests the emotional aspect of empathy, not the cognitive one. He says there's a significant difference between feeling for someone and being able to put yourself in their shoes.'

'Is that right?'

'Yes,' says his father, watching as Óli jacks up the car. 'And he says, moreover, that you can't really talk about an "empathy test" because empathy is both of these things combined.'

'Interesting.'

His father looks at him and shakes his head with a disapproving expression. Óli picks the wrench up again and starts loosening the wheel nuts all the way.

'This is just foolishness, Óli. It's a power play and nothing else. There's a zero per cent chance that this test will make society better in any way, I guarantee you that.'

He bats his hand when Óli starts nudging the tyre off, gesturing for him to move aside.

'You keep going with that one,' he says and takes over, wiggling the flat tyre off and the new one on, before screwing the wheel nuts back on by hand. Óli moves to the next tyre. They work in silence.

'Bingo,' says his father when they've finished. Óli jacks the car back down and tightens all the wheel nuts as much as he can.

'I'll take these,' says his father, pointing to the old tyres.

'Yeah? Are you sure?'

'Já, já, it's on my way.'

The tyre repair shop is actually in the opposite direction. His father picks up two of the tyres and flings them in the back of his truck. Óli follows with the other two.

'Jæja, I'll head out now,' says his father then. 'Has Dagný left for preschool? Or is she still upstairs?'

'Sólveig has already taken her.'

'Ah. I was thinking I could take her.'

'I'm sure she would have loved that.'

His father nods, gets in his truck. Rolls down the window and backs out of the drive.

'Thanks for the help, Dad.'

His father raises his hand in farewell and drives away.

Sólveig is watching a video when he comes inside. He doesn't take off his jacket. Himnar will be there any minute to pick him up.

'Have you seen this?'

She enlarges her screen with a flick of her fingers. He goes over and rubs her back, puts his arms around her, kisses her cheek.

At first, he thinks he's watching a PSYCH video. The background, the colours, the set – they're all the same. The boy can't be much over twenty; his cheeks are peppered with acne. His mouth sags half-open, giving him a witless air. His Icelandic is horrific – awful grammar, riddled with slang – but he seems aware of it and repeats some words twice, even three times, as if his mother tongue is a slippery bar of soap he can't keep hold of. The boy is talking about his childhood and troubles at home, says a specialist put his brother on trex, to help the brother develop his empathetic abilities. The boy himself is now addicted to it. He says trex has had terrible repercussions for him. His vision is now impaired, for one.

A voice behind the camera asks how the boy sees the future. What his plans are. The boy says the residents of the building he lives in have started collecting signatures in favour of having it marked and that the rental office will not be renewing his lease. He's going to be thrown out in a few weeks. He wants to buy an apartment, so he'll be safe. If he fails the test, the bank won't give him a loan and no one will rent him an apartment, either.

The video ends and he gets a call. It's Salóme.

'And so it begins,' says Sólveig.

'It looks like one of ours.'

'Yes, but why?'

'So that people think he went into treatment. And then they see this.'

'They've got to be targeting marked people with this.'

'Without a doubt.'

'They must have more of them.'

'What should we do?'

'We don't pay any attention to it. We'll just put more money into getting our own stories out there.'

'When you've been knocking at a door for X amount of time,' says a boy in a new MASC video on Wednesday, 'and no one opens it and you finally realise that they're never going to let you in, you start looking for a window to break. That's just the way it is.'

'I experienced some trauma in my childhood,' says an elegant woman around fifty. 'The doctors say that's why I failed. I've been in treatment for two years, but it's not having any of the intended results. The Psychological Association refuses to grant me an exception. This has completely ruined my life. I was fired from my job and have since developed an alcohol problem. My marriage couldn't take the stress, and my husband moved out. My youngest asks me on a regular basis if I'm going to jail.'

'These are real people's stories,' says Magnús Geirsson. 'These aren't bad people. These aren't lesser people. These people are just people like the rest of us, and they deserve the same opportunities and the same access as everyone else.'

Óli explains the situation to Sólveig. He's going to need to work overtime in the coming days.

'It's always the same story,' she says.

'Just one more month, then it's over,' he pleads.

Dagný yelps from the bathroom that she's finished and Sólveig walks out, leaving him alone in the kitchen.

The latest figures are published on Friday. Sixty per cent in favour.

'Do you think it's the videos?' asks Himnar.

'It doesn't have to mean anything,' says Salóme. 'This is just one poll of many. By next week, we could be back up to sixty-five per cent.'

All of the prediction models anticipate that support will drop as they get closer to the referendum. They're hoping for sixty per cent during referendum week itself.

Óli takes a seat and starts to plan out the coming week, scheduling visits and interviews. Himnar is whistling a ditty behind him, the same refrain over and over.

'Can you stop whistling?' says Óli, as calmly as he can.

'Sorry,' says Himnar.

Óli stands up, gets a soda water, and tries to massage the fatigue from his face. He never meant to get involved in politics. He associates politics with his father. He made a point of absenting himself whenever his father and his fellow partisans offered him a seat at the kitchen table, where they sat agreeing that the opposition were opportunistic good-for-nothings. He felt outright defiant whenever he heard them singing his praises. Saying what a promising young man he'd turned out to be.

'When women speak ill of other people,' said his mum at the time, 'it's called gossip. But when men speak ill of other people, it's called politics.'

When Óli first became involved in university politics, his father was thrilled, even though one of his campaign issues was increasing psychological services for students. He asked about the elections every night, and cheered Óli on like a football dad. It was clearly needed, when you thought about it, Óli heard him say to his comrades. Kids had become so confounded anxious these days, they carried the whole world on their shoulders.

But his father and his friends dragged their heels when it came to mental health issues. Psychological services were okay, but the mark, taking a test to prove one's merit – this they wrote off as a passing fad, a trendy wave. They joked about it constantly until that wave crashed into Alþingi, and it was only then – far too late – that they waded into the surf. Suddenly, his father's kitchen-table lectures started being directed at Óli. By that point, though, Óli had long since stopped responding to him; he couldn't understand why his sister bothered to argue with him night after night. You couldn't debate their father – he'd just interrupt you or mock whatever you said. But even so, Óli started using his father's opinions to bolster his own. He kept his mouth shut and listened, considered his father's opinions from all angles, held them up to the light, so that anytime he encountered the same arguments elsewhere, he was ready, outspoken and unhesitating.

The interviewer introduces himself, but Óli doesn't catch his name. A little camera flits around them and then hovers motionless in the air beside them like a third conversant.

'What's PSYCH's take on the new videos that MASC has been releasing over these past few weeks? It could be claimed that these videos call for more empathy to be shown to precisely those whom the test appears to cast out of society.'

'It goes without saying that these people need assistance,' says Óli. 'And assistance is available to them, whenever they want it. That's why I don't use words like "cast out", but rather words like "integrate". From my perspective, these individuals have elected not to participate in society. But even so, treatment isn't some cure-all that is going to fix everything in a single night. Treatment like this takes time – months, maybe years. These are often lonely people who don't have the tools to work on themselves. We want to heal people who are suffering from illness and offer them a healthy future.'

'But what if these people don't want help?'

'Then they don't take it. There's no one forcing anyone to do anything. But it's important that the offer of help stands. Free, and without obligation, whenever they so choose. I think it's a fair demand that those who want to take part in this project we call society show that they are capable of doing so. The marking mandate isn't just a way for us to create a safer society, it's also financially beneficial for the state. As can be seen both here and in neighbouring countries. Criminal offences are very costly for society. One broken person can break ten other people in quite a short amount of time. Violence costs us in healthcare services and disability compensation. And we simply can't afford it any more.'

Himnar gives him a ride home. They're both tired and don't talk. Óli replays the interview in his head, runs back over what he said. How he said it, whether he came off as arrogant. He projects the video in front of him and Himnar watches out of the corner of his eye.

No, he was measured and polite. He wore a neutral smile and somehow managed to come off as both humble and firm.

Then he opens the news and sees Magnús Geirsson's face.

'What's he saying now?' asks Himnar.

'Nothing new, I don't think. "These poor boys are the ones who lose out," something like that.'

'It's poetic, don't you think, that the man who gave us the term "loser morality" is now so concerned with who loses?' says Himnar. 'Remember that whole year when all he talked about was how society was coddling crybabies who just wanted to whine about everything?'

'I do.'

'We ought to put out a dictionary to explain what men like Magnús Geirsson actually mean. That sentimentality means emotional intelligence, whining means criticism, and hysteria repercussions.'

Óli smiles companionably at his friend. He leans his head back and closes his eyes.

Himnar pulls into the driveway and Óli gets out.

'How d'you feel about taking over on Monday?' asks Himnar.

'Great, of course,' says Óli. 'I'll pick you up at nine.'

As he shuts the car door behind him, he notices the boy. He's wearing a black hoodie and is half-hidden behind a jeep that's parked down the street. He's got one hand raised, as though he's taking a picture or a video with his watch.

Himnar drives off. Óli acts like nothing's amiss, walks calmly up the stairs and into the house. Once he's inside, he calls the policewoman and describes the boy. She says she'll send a car right away. He peeks out the window as surreptitiously as he can. The boy crouches there for a few more seconds before striding away, looking to both sides and hefting his backpack on his shoulders. For a moment, Óli considers following him. But then he remembers the tyres. The boy might have a knife. Óli paces, runs his hands through his hair until they are sticky with pomade. He goes into the bathroom and washes his hands. Then he waits.

12.

Tristan tells Zoé to give him directions to the building, then he puts on something upbeat and walks in time with the song. *Right*, says Zoé over the music when he should turn right, *Left*, when he should turn left. Once he's in the neighbourhood, he starts looking around. There are a lot of really big trees here, little paths between the streets, no loud-arse highway right outside your bedroom window. It's a teeny tiny little street-level unit built into a hillside, half the apartment is basically buried, no windows or anything. But the side that's not buried is mega nice. There's a big garden that the agent says faces south and the view is awesome because the hillside keeps going down so you look right onto the roof of the house below and then there's a paved corner by the patio door that the agent says is totally sheltered from the wind.

Some of the people checking the place out look like they hate it for all intensive purposes. People his mum would call 'the less fortunate' and pretend she was better than even though she's just as fucking poor and has it just as fucking hard. Someone asks the agent if it would be okay to underbid a little.

'So, there's a lot of a demand for properties like this right now,' says the agent. 'Most people overbid, at least in the first twenty-four hours.'

Tristan glances at the agent. He looks exactly like a player on the national football team. Like, exactly like him.

'Oh yeah?' says the man who asked. He's Latino or something like that and he's wearing a big, black leather jacket.

'Yes, these apartments that have private entrances or are on unmarked floors. People are giving themselves a bit of insurance, before the referendum.'

'Wait a sec, weren't you on the football team?' asks the Latino guy.

'Yes,' says the agent curtly and turns away.

The next day, Tristan calls the agent and says he wants to make an offer. The agent says, Great, and that he'll call him back later, but he doesn't. Tristan knows it probably isn't personal, but it still makes him feel super stressed the next day when he thinks about calling again so he decides to just go to the bank instead to see if maybe they can make an offer for him or something. When he walks in, there's a cool hologram AI that says, *Good afternoon, Tristan*, and then, *How can we help you today?* and he says he wants to get a loan for an apartment.

Wonderful, says the AI. Tristan tries to figure out if the AI is a woman or a man, but it's kinda both. It has both a beard and long, dark eyelashes. The AI invites him to sit on a bench and he does.

Tristan, you're registered as single and unmarked, no children, no debt, no property. Is that correct?

'Yeah.'

Wonderful. Have you found a property you would like to make an offer on?

'Yeah, this one.' He projects it up between them.

Wonderful. I see that your equity here will cover up to 13.41 per cent of the value of the property, but in order to be granted a loan of more than eighty per cent, you will need to take our empathy test.

'What? But last time it was eighty-five per cent.'

New regulations went into effect on the first of February. We do not require our patrons to mark themselves in the PSYCH database at the end of the test. Your results are for our records only and will be kept confidential.

'But I've got to buy an apartment before the fucking vote!!'

The AI says nothing.

'Okay, but then what about other stuff? Other loans??'

Unfortunately, that will not be possible, Tristan. Per regulation 666/2042, which was set by the Financial Supervisory Authority concerning mortgage maximums on property purchased by individuals, only eighty per cent of the market value of the property may be loaned to the borrower if the individual in question is unmarked.

'Fuck! Come ON, I'm a human being! I work full-time!'

According to a report published by the Financial Supervisory Authority, seventy-two per cent of properties that go into bankruptcy are owned by unmarked individuals.

'But I've got to buy an apartment!' he says. His voice has started shaking and his hands are trembling and his body, too. 'Don't you get that? I've got to get my own apartment before this fucking vote happens!'

The AI says nothing.

'Is there a person here I can talk to? A real person?'

Our customer service agents work from our branch office on Mondays and Wednesdays. Would you like to book an appointment and come back next week?

'Yeah, book me an appointment, fine.'

Of course.

'How much more money do I need to be able to make a fucking twenty per cent down payment?'

The AI tells him. He stands up and leaves. As he walks up the hill and past the statue of Ingólfur Arnarson, he works out how long it would take him to save another five per cent for a down payment. At least five fucking months. If he like, really, really saves.

When he walks past the shop on his way to Eldór's, the facial-recognition reader screams at him: EE EE EE.

'I'm not even trying to go in!!' he says, yanking on the door to Eldór's building. The hall is carpeted and windowless and smells dusty. They sit out on the balcony and smoke the *jurt* Eldór always has. Tristan tells him about his bank visit.

'Nei, have some more,' says Eldór when Tristan tries to pass the j back to him.

Then they're both real quiet while they wait for it to hit.

'Just think about it,' says Eldór out of nowhere. 'This was a hotel for literally decades or something. Just think how many people have slept here.'

Eldór's voice is getting slow. Tristan tries to look at him, but his head is too heavy.

'Just think about how many people have fucked in my bedroom,' he hears Eldór say. 'So many people who are dead fucked here once. It's wild, man. It's like there's some huge ghost parade marching through my room.'

Tristan is caught up in his own thoughts. It's like his body is a giant pool and he's just a little body in that pool and when he holds his breath, he can float, but he starts sinking whenever he breathes out.

'. . . we could talk to Viktor . . .' says Eldór and his voice is slow and thick, like he's sleeping. '. . . help out with the next container . . . if we could clean a few houses . . . then maybe you'd be able to save enough . . . I could get us a car . . . if you take the car and do the cleaning yourself . . . I can't be around anything like that right now . . . because of the probation, þú veist . . .' His mouth is open and his eyes are half-closed. He lifts both hands and looks from one watch to another. '. . . three more months . . . in three more months I'm a free man . . . no Spotter . . . no paranoia . . .'

Tristan tries to turn his head to answer but when he does, his head flops onto his shoulder. When did it get so heavy? His head is insanely fucking heavy. He tries to lift it again, to lean it back on the wall, but his hands are too heavy, too. They hang down by his sides and there's a nice tingling feeling in them. Super nice. He thinks about Sunneva. Why'd he have to fuck it up with Sunneva? She was like light. He'd never kissed light before he kissed her. He'd never slept with light before he slept with her. She could have been his girl-friend. He could have seen her every day and slept next to her at night and not always been alone.

'. . . yeah . . .' he hears Eldór say. '. . . five . . . houses . . . cool.'

Eldór talks to Viktor and Viktor says they can help with the next container and Eldór finds them a big car and Tristan asks if he can leave work at lunch the next day and Viktor says yes.

In the morning, Tristan takes his good clothes to work with him and puts them on at lunch. He takes the S straight to Eldór's and scrolls through a discussion thread and comments on the way.

And theres loads of UNREFUTABLE evidence that shows that people who take the test BUT DONT MAKR THEMSELVES are put on the govt register ANYWAY amd that they have to deal w all kinds of CUTBACKS and DISCRIMINATION like benefit cuts and les opportunitys if they dont mark themselvs !! This is the 1 true goal of the majority: to create an OPPRESIVE state wherein the minority is BRUTALLY PUNISHED. 1st they establish 'TREATMENT RESORCES' and then next thing you know that becomes 'REEDUCATION CAMPS' and where does it stop?? In CONSENTRATION CAMPS!! NEI !! we SHALL NOT stand by!! We will ALWAYS defend our HUAMN RIGHTS!

the other thing they do is they pick you up, lock you in a cell, and say either you take the test or well arrest you for reals and then if they dont like you adn you say no then they just charge you with some madeup thing that makes no sens and its just their word against yours this happened to my buddy and they made him take the test when he was totally fucked up on OP and of corse he failed and then they were able to get a judge to give him a longer sentence and fine him more

fucking pigs

just come to spain amigos :-) none of this bullshit, just cheap food and cheap houses, and then you can just fuck off back home for the hottest part of the summer ;-)

He asks Zoé to play some calming piano music and sits there with his eyes closed for a while but then an ad interrupts out of nowhere and he opens his eyes thinking he's going to see the fucking face of one of those fucking PSYCH guys and he feels all his muscles clenching but when he opens his eyes, it isn't Ólafur Tandri or Himnar Þór, but him. It's his own face, way, way too big and close. He had no idea his face would be up close like this. It's really weird seeing yourself so big on a screen. He scrolls down and sees that there are comments under the video, like, a lot of comments, ninety or something. He asks Zoé to read the comments and closes his eyes and listens. Someone wishes him all the best and someone else says he doesn't deserve this and a third commenter says it's horrible to see how society is treating young men these days. He listens to comment after comment and his throat starts hurting and he feels the muscles in his face get all stiff and he's about to start fucking crying right here on the S-line, with all these people around.

He stands up and tells Zoé to play something more upbeat and then he hops off the S and picks up the car that Eldór left in a parking garage that doesn't have any cameras, or at least no cameras the cops can get into.

He drives up to Kópavogur to this ugly, old apartment complex, and stops in front of a green building. He looks around for one of those stickers – a circle with a big M inside it – but all he sees is a rusty silver sign that says that some woman lived here from 1997 to 2015. He projects a holomask with a filter that changes his face. The intercom is old, too. No face recognition or voice recognition or fingerprints or anything. He reads the mailboxes and decides to be Aron Hafliði from the second floor, if someone asks. He's on high alert, super wired and focused, like he always gets when he cleans. He tries to control his body, the shaking, closes his eyes for a moment and then starts at the top, presses the bell for 601. No answer. Good. He presses 602. Nothing. He rings all the bells on the fifth floor. Finally, someone in 403 answers and he looks straight into the camera when he introduces himself as Aron and makes sure his clean, collared shirt is visible when he says he accidentally locked himself out when he was running out to get a bag from the car. He lifts up the bag he's holding.

Sure, no problem, says the woman. The door opens and

he's in. He takes the elevator straight to the seventh floor where there's no one home and looks at himself in the mirror. The holomask has moved his eyes closer together, his mouth lower and made his jaw wider.

The elevator helps him calm down. He feels good in elevators. There's something dead-arse comforting about them. When he and Rúrik were little, they would often play in the elevator in their old apartment building, one of them would run up and down the stairs trying to beat the elevator, maybe press all the buttons on the way to slow the other one down. When he's insanely stressed, he likes to tell himself he's in an elevator. He's in an elevator and he can't go any faster.

The lock is old and it takes him less than two minutes to get into the apartment.

'Halló?' he says.

No answer. He closes the door behind him and tiptoes slowly out of the mud room. This place has high ceilings and an open staircase in the middle that goes upstairs. He starts in the living room, there are, like, ten guitars and a few amps, all super fucking expensive shit. But first he deactivates his holomask. Then he goes into the office and there are all these computers and equipment, a drone and a fancy printer, he jumbles all of it in the mud room then goes up to the bedroom, finds the most expensive clothes and jewellery in the dresser, takes them. He has to make a few trips back and forth from the apartment to the elevator and then just as many trips from the elevator to the boot of the car, and he tries his best to keep his body relaxed and act like he lives there. He closes the boot and goes back up for the guitars. There's something wrong about stealing instruments, they're so personal somehow. But what does one person need with ten fucking guitars? That's not healthy for anyone. He takes the elevator back up, walks straight into the living room, and takes three guitars, the shiniest ones that look like they're barely used, and then he closes the door behind him and gets the fuck out of there.

He takes the car to another parking garage, where he moves the stuff into a different car that he drives to a third garage. He leaves it there with all the shit in it. Eldór will pick it up tonight and drive it out to the countryside.

He takes the H-line and transfers to the S and reads the new comments that are under the video now. 'Give this poor young man a chance,' someone writes. 'Good luck, Tristan,' writes someone else. 'I feel for the kid, of course, but anyone can see he needs a psychologist,' writes some woman under that and links to treatment resources in her comment.

That makes him really fucking mad when he reads that, and he clicks on her picture. She looks like your typical therapy bitch, with old-fashioned glasses and grey streaks in her hair. He blocks her, even though he doesn't even know her.

He gets off at his stop and keeps listening to Zoé reading the comments. He walks past the corner and automatically looks up the street towards Ólafur Tandri's house. The car has new tyres. Just then, Ólafur Tandri gets out of a different car that's parked in front of the house and Tristan hides behind a big jeep and without thinking about it, lifts his hand and turns on the camera and zooms in on Ólafur Tandri and records him walking into his house.

Tristan waits for a moment before he keeps going down the street, thinking about what he's going to write to go with the video when he sends it later. Last time, he wrote such brutal fucking shit that he made himself sick, when he talked about poking their eyes out and stuff. He's going to say 'we' like he did last time, like there are tons of people watching Ólafur Tandri, and he hopes he wakes up in the morning with fucking stomach pains and feels like he's not safe.

Tristan is literally almost all the way home when the cop car drives up the street towards him. He automatically looks down and tries to walk slowly, act normal. Then he hears the siren, just one whoop, not full blast, like they want him to know they're coming for him, and he freezes. A whole bunch of thoughts attack his brain at the same time: they followed him from Kópavogur. He's going to jail. He won't get to buy an apartment. He won't get to date Sunneva. He will never be normal.

The cop car stops in front of him. Right in the same second the door opens, he gets this insanely strong urge to run, to just get the fuck out of there, maybe they haven't seen his face. But then the cops slam the doors and look right at him, and so he just stands there on the pavement and when the cops start talking, he doesn't hear anything and when one of them takes his arm and pulls him towards the car, his feet obey and walk to the car and not in the other direction and not home.

13.

And then the day comes, the day her class takes the test. Vetur lies in bed inert until the last possible moment instead of eating a good breakfast like she planned, or taking a shower like she planned, she stays there until she has to leave in a rush. She walks as fast as she can without actually breaking into a run, the sky is dotted with white clouds, the air humid, the streets are wet and saturated with cars making their way to work.

A steady stream of people is going in and out of the gate and a few metres away several cars are nosing into the underground parking garage as others inch out of it in the opposite direction. The distance between the pedestrian and the car entrances is short, twenty, maybe thirty metres at most. Then her unconscious hooks onto something that makes her heart shrink, she turns so fast she pulls a muscle in her neck, she feels the blood running down into her shoulders to the locus of the pain, and then, as if she's floating outside her body, she catches sight of a car in the middle of the queue into the neighbourhood, a black car she recognises.

It's him. He's sitting nonchalantly in the Benz, looking at the car ahead of him. And then, as if he can sense someone watching him, he turns his head, looks straight at her, his dark eyes neutral, distant. Gravity becomes heavier, something pulls her down, pins and needles begin to surge through her arms and down her thighs, across her cheeks and jaw, Daníel's expression changes from disinterest to shock, she looks away too fast, as if she hasn't seen anything, she's got to get to the gate, she's got to get through the gate, and then she's made it to the other side, but relief doesn't take hold like it usually does, she looks back and sees the boot of the car disappearing down into the garage, he's also made it through, which means this neighbourhood isn't safe any more. She isn't safe any more.

But he failed, he had to have failed. He didn't come back to school after the staff was tested, he resigned due to serious illness, which means fail, everyone knows that, anything evasive means fail, anything people don't talk about means fail, and 'serious illness' is both evasive and something people don't talk about. She scurries on, overtaking people on the pavement, his hair was cut short, he was alone in the car, he was wearing a nice blazer, he must be working here, he must be on his way to work, why else would he be here at a quarter to nine in the morning?

She arrives at school and huddles in a corridor, flicks up her projector and navigates to one of the daily papers, scrolls through the news without taking in any of the headlines, snaps out of it, opens her mailbox, looks for something to hold on to, opens a gram she finds from the headmistress, doesn't take in anything, and by then, it's nine o'clock and the bell rings for class. Húnbogi comes up to her where she's

140

standing amid a stream of students, still in her coat, dishev-elled, absent-minded, he says something, but she's in a fog.

She asks Zoé to pull up her class's schedule. They're cur-rently one floor down; she takes the stairs, inhales deeply, unbuttons her coat and drapes it over one arm, brushes the hair from her face, opens the door a crack, smiles, and points for the nearest boy to come with her. The boy looks at his seatmate, an anxious smile on his lips, and then follows her out. Vetur knocks on the door to the little lounge and says good morning to the team. The team greets them warmly, the boy is beckoned into the room with a friendly gesture, to a chair in the middle of the room. A thin, glass helmet is resting on the seat.

'This usually takes about fifteen minutes,' says one of the psychologists and then the door closes, Vetur sits on the bench outside the room and asks Zoé to look Daníel up in the Registry and a second later, she's looking at words she can't absorb, doesn't understand. She asks what it says.

Daníel Arason, pass, says Zoé.

She folds over, holds her head, tries to get her bearings, focuses on her breathing, closes her eyes and the black Benz appears; Daníel is sitting in the driver's seat and moving things from the passenger seat to the back just before she gets in the car and gives him a kiss.

She knew he wasn't her final destination, just like she knew her relationship with the attractive woman wasn't her final destination, nor her fling with the tall bass player before that.

And yet she allowed his hopes to mushroom from one day to the next. She fed on him like a parasite, like a flea on a starling, he said she was the most beautiful girl he'd ever seen and when she looked in the mirror, she saw this beautiful girl, saw herself the way he saw her. Every time he opened up was a victory, to have broken through that reserve, to have seen something that only a chosen few had seen, and then she watered him like a flower, paid him more and more attention in order to see deeper and deeper inside him.

Little by little, he started saying all kinds of things in the dark after they slept together. That he couldn't believe this was happening. That he'd given up on finding someone. That he was waking up to life.

She's nauseous. How long has he been roaming around the neighbourhood, driving past her? And how? He's not allowed to get so close to her, the police are notified whenever he gets within twenty metres. But he was so close . . . was it he who had rattled her doorknob? Her arms go weak. With great effort, she sends a gram to her psychologist and asks her to call back as soon as possible. She sends a gram to her girlfriends, spluttering out the words, then to her parents, and then, finally, to the legal advocate who took care of the restraining order, asks her to call when she has a chance.

After a few minutes, she goes down to the natural sciences room to get the next boy. The door to the testing room opens, one boy comes out and another goes in.

—

There was a point at which she looked at him and thought: Maybe. He had beautiful dark eyes and sinewy hands that she could easily imagine holding a child. There was no reason not to meet up on Fridays after class, get a drink together, have dinner together, end the evening back at her place. There was no reason not to invite him to lunch the next day, to go to the pool together after lunch, no reason for him not to stick around after the pool, to order a pizza, watch a TV show at hers or spend the night together like any other couple.

But when her girlfriends encouraged her to bring him to dinner parties, she hesitated. When her parents asked if she had a special someone, she hesitated. When he invited her to his hometown for a weekend, she found a way out of it. Maybe because she could tell that something wasn't entirely right. Sometimes she caught a glimpse of something ugly, something hard: if he faced the slightest resistance, he immediately got defensive, and not just defensive, more like claws out and hissing. She came to understand very quickly that he couldn't deal with banter of even the mildest sort; if she disagreed with him, she wasn't supposed to raise any objections, but rather change the subject entirely. He began saying worse and worse things about their co-workers. He said he couldn't understand how some of their colleagues could have university degrees, that the idea of certain colleagues reproducing gave him chills, said that whenever Ýmir Nóri, the assistant headmaster, opened his mouth, he felt every cell in his body committing suicide, putrefying inside him, that he never felt quite so much like he was wasting his life as when he was sitting with their co-workers at lunch and listening to their vapid, bourgeois yapping.

A co-worker whose name she can't remember walks by with a cup of coffee and a jangling keyring, slows down and asks if everything's okay.

'Já, já,' says Vetur, looking up. 'Ache. I mean, headache. I mean, I'm getting a migraine.'

'Ugh,' says her co-worker with a sympathetic grimace.

She plods upstairs and down, ferrying the kids to and from the test, some silent and some loud, Vetur gives them permission to call their parents, she takes her coffee break, snaps to attention mid-conversation, mid-question and answers the best she can.

He never pushed her for more time, never brought up the fact that they didn't see each other on weeknights, sensed that he should keep a friendly distance during working hours. If he was frustrated or hurt, he didn't show it.

In the beginning, she'd liked Daníel's contemptuousness, he seemed aware of it, and didn't seem to take himself too seriously. He'd clearly been an outcast his whole life, *persona non grata*, maybe not the victim of bullying per se, but definitely not popular, and Vetur thought it was to be expected that this was how he'd vindicate himself, that the near friendlessness was a choice he made, that he wouldn't have any hobbies and was satisfied with two best friends, the internet, video games, TV shows, and music. But the less he censored himself, the more she started realising that he probably had been bullied, or at the very least, excluded socially. He told her about the time someone at school held the door open for two people but let it close on him. He told her about the time the assistant headmaster remarked (understandably) on his habitual sick days. He told her about the time the division head asked him to work something into his curriculum, as if he hadn't done that ages ago, as if he didn't know how to do his job.

She witnessed him interpret the most ludicrous comments as attacks or as scorn, the most innocuous interactions as hostile or malicious. She learned to read in his face whether he'd shut someone out or not, learned to see when he'd taken offence – when his eyes went dead and his sentences became monotonous. He never reacted when he felt like he was being talked down to, just said Okay and then carried around all his contempt and hatred until Friday, when he'd ask Vetur if she'd noticed when someone said This or someone else said That.

She tried to be patient, to be a diplomat. She gently came to their co-workers' defence, said this or that person probably hadn't meant it like that, Daníel shouldn't get himself so worked up over nothing. Then she stopped bothering; she just kept silent while he gossiped or else abruptly changed the subject, interrupted him even, in the hope that he would knock it off. But then came the moment one Friday night, when he was sitting at the kitchen table and said, Guess what Ýmir Nóri said today, and Vetur sighed, put the knife down on the cutting board and said, What did he say now, Daníel? and then watched as the words congealed in his throat, as his body stiffened, and, with a practised, polite coldness, said, Nothing, never mind.

The kids have Maths after the break. Vetur opens the class-room door a crack and meets Tildra's eyes. She gestures for her to come.

'Can Naómí come with me?' asks Tildra.

Vetur hesitates and looks at Naómí. 'Já, já,' she says.

Both girls stand up. Naómí brings her apple with her.

'I'm so nervous,' says Tildra, her shoulders hunched up to her ears.

Naómí doesn't say anything.

'It's going to be fine,' says Vetur.

'It's so unfair that people who live here have to do this,' says Tildra. 'If we fail, we might have to move. People who don't live in marked neighbourhoods don't have to worry about it at all.'

Vetur doesn't respond. They've reached the testing room. Tildra goes in and the student who comes out pads back to class. Vetur and Naómí sit on chairs outside the room. Naómí is expressionless, looks down at the apple she's hold-ing, cuts a half-moon in the green skin with her thumbnail. The minutes pass in silence.

'Vetur,' says Naómí abruptly, still not looking up, 'I don't want to take the test. I want to call it off.'

Vetur looks at her.

'That's not an option, unfortunately,' Vetur says, as delicately as she can.

'But I'm so scared,' says Naómí, and her voice cracks, her eyes fill with tears. 'I don't want to take it. I can't take it.'

Vetur places a hand on her shoulder and in the same moment, Naómí starts sobbing.

'This is just something that we all have to do. There are rules in this neighbourhood. It's not a big deal. I promise.'

'It's so unfair,' says Naómí.

'You have nothing to worry about,' says Vetur. 'Worst-case scenario, you'll just meet with your psychologist more often.'

Naómí's tears subside, and she starts sniffling, drying her eyes with her sweatshirt. The door to the testing room opens. Tildra sees Naómí and puts her arms around her, tells her it's no big deal. The embrace evokes another sob and when they release one another, Naómí squares her shoulders, looks up into the air, exhales, dries her tears with the hand that's holding the apple, and disappears through the open door.

14.

Kári calls her on Monday.

Says he found a fountain pen in his office.

Þórir's pen. Under his desk.

'What?' she says.

'Are you serious?' she says.

'You don't think . . . Þórir is spying on you?'

Kári says he heard a rumour the other day. That Þórir is taking credit for his contract negotiations. With the power plant in Japan.

It's all really uncomfortable.

'Gosh. I can believe it,' she says. 'What are you going to do?'

Kári says he doesn't know. He's going to think about it.

Every day, there are new articles about Fjölnir and his business history.

An old bankruptcy.

An *ancient* fishing quota dispute that turned out not to be a criminal matter.

She gets calls from reporters asking about their working relationship. Whether there have been any suspicious or questionable dealings.

—

The pills make her feel like she's had two glasses of red wine.

Like everything is . . . lovely. Like she's floating.

She asks Gylfi to come over and do different things from usual.

She asks him to lie on top of her and touch her everywhere.

But sometimes she feels completely lost.

She starts to tear up over stupid things. Her dad. Her mum. Breki.

She stops taking the pills for two, three days.

Fjölnir finally calls her back.

He says Þórir was obviously waiting for this. As soon as Þórir figured out that Alli also knew Fjölnir's test results, he was free to leak it to the media, since he wasn't the only person it could be traced back to any more. Þórir must have been over the moon the two of them showed up together. He'd been playing the long game.

'Jesus Christ,' she says. 'This is disgraceful.'

Já, says Fjölnir. That it is.

'I just don't know if I want to keep working under that man,' she says. 'Maybe it's time to start looking around for something else.'

Fjölnir says it would be way too suspicious to switch companies now. She's got to wait at least a year. Unless she moves to a firm that's marked.

'Yeah, you're probably right,' she answers.

'Maybe I can stick out the year,' she says. 'Though I hate to do it.'

She makes a decision.

She confers with Gylfi and sets up a remote meeting with EcoZea, the company that makes the filter motor.

She tells them that something's come up at her firm.

A moral issue.

She's transferring to a new firm and they're interested in buying shares, just like her last company, but the new firm will make a better offer.

The owners of EcoZea are young, a man and a woman; they're both cautious and earnest.

She makes them an offer.

They say they need time to consider but will let her know, no later than next week.

She takes two pills instead of one the next morning.

She feels light-headed as she walks across the car park to the white building.

In the reception area, an AI tells her to take a seat in the waiting room.

In the waiting room, there's another woman around her age wearing a herringbone coat.

The waiting room is cosy. Painted trendy colours.

Soft leather sofas. A pendant lamp over the coffee table.

She leans back; that familiar euphoria flows through her body.

She touches the empty cushion next to her.

Bright. It's way too bright.

She looks for her sunglasses in her purse but doesn't find them.

The woman in the herringbone coat is sitting with her head bent.

There's something so . . . terribly sad about her expression.

'I'm so sorry,' she hears herself say.

The woman looks up and then at Eyja when she realises the words were directed at her.

'For what?' asks the woman. Her voice is sharp and transparent; suddenly, Eyja can hear the feelings in her voice. She picks up false politeness, suspicion and impatience.

'I don't know. But I'm really sorry, for whatever it is.'

Then a girl appears from one of the rooms.

'Eyja?'

She stands up; her head feels so light. She walks slowly towards the girl.

'Is this your first time here, Eyja?'

Eyja looks at the girl, at her big, blue eyes, her buck teeth.

'Sorry . . . what did you say?' asks Eyja.

'Is this your first time here?' asks the girl.

Eyja watches the girl's mouth as it moves. It's like she has direct access to the girl's voice . . . like an electrical cord plugged into a socket.

'Are you okay?' asks the girl, taking Eyja's shoulder as if she thinks she's about to fall.

'Yes . . .' she says. 'I'm just . . . sensitive today.'

She rubs her eyes. She needs to focus.

'Take as much time as you need. It's normal to feel anxious.'

Eyja looks at her. The girl's words echo inside her. She feels something click into place and suddenly a feeling unfurls in her, enlarges. She can't get hold of the feeling. A thought comes to her, as though from somewhere else, outside of her: Many houses make a city.

'You can take a seat here, Eyja. When you're ready.'

'Thanks. Thank you kindly,' she says and sits in a big leather chair and the girl removes the watches from her wrists and wraps plastic straps in their place. Then a large helmet is placed on her head.

'We're going to play a few videos for you. You don't have to do anything but watch and listen. There's a button here if you need to stop or take a break.'

The girl steps outside and after a few moments, a middle-aged man's face appears on the inside of the helmet. Eyja can make out every tiny detail on his face: the pores on his nose, the shine where he's recently shaved, the swelling around his chin. The saggy bags under his eyebrows.

Another thought comes to her: Context.

The man looks into her eyes, his expression neutral. Then, slowly but surely, his eyes become more and more distressed, the shape of his mouth more forlorn. His face crumples and he bursts into tears. He holds his face and cries.

Eyja tries to mirror his expression. Two tears spring from her eyes. They trickle down her cheeks.

Two tears. That's more than last time.

Then the video cuts to a woman, maybe around twenty.

She goes through the same motions. Looks at the camera until she starts to cry.

Cut. A Black woman in her thirties cries.

Cut. An East Asian man in his seventies cries.

Cut. A woman in a niqab cries.

Every video is roughly a minute long. Then a little boy appears, maybe seven years old. He looks at the camera and then starts to smile. He smiles wider and wider until he bursts into shrieking laughter. He leans his head back and laughs, mouth open, so she can see all the way to his uvula. His nostrils flutter.

Cut. The first man laughs.

Cut. The twenty-year-old woman laughs.

Cut. The East Asian man laughs. His shoulders shake with merriment.

Cut. A blond woman between thirty and forty looks at the camera and talks about having several miscarriages and then losing a baby in childbirth.

Cut. A Black woman talks about her daughter being mis-diagnosed with the flu when what she actually had was a rare form of leukaemia. She died seven months later.

Cut. A young, dark-haired Arab man talks about fleeing across the ocean with his mother and sister after his father was shot outside their home. He recalls how the boat cap-sized, how he and his mother spent many weeks searching for his fourteen-year-old sister's body on the beach.

She *should* cry.

She *should* pity them.

It's hard.

After a few more stories, the girl comes in and unfastens the bands around her wrists. She tells Eyja she can expect her results the next day.

Eyja goes home and falls asleep and wakes up seventeen hours later.

She can barely move.

She turns on the feature that disguises her voice and makes her phone calls untraceable and calls the twenty-four-hour medical hotline.

She tells the doctor she took two Oxym yesterday.

The doctor is impassive when he tells her she can thank her lucky stars that she didn't fall into a coma or experience a psychotic episode. He asks if she's using daily.

'Using?' she repeats.

'I just started taking it,' she says.

'Isn't this supposed to make you more empathetic?'

The doctor says the recommended dosage is one pill a week, alongside intensive psychological treatment. Oxym does boost the production of oxytocin, but it's primarily taken to force nerve impulses to forge new pathways in the brain, unclog blockages.

The delivery service has left three smoothies outside her door.

She sits on the sofa with one of the smoothies and asks Zoé to open her medical portal.

Emotional Transmission, Joy: Normal response.

Emotional Transmission, Friendship: Normal response.

Emotional Transmission, Pain: Does not demonstrate minimum response.

Pain of Others (Same Gender): Does not demonstrate minimum response.

Pain of Others (Different Gender): Does not demonstrate minimum response.

Pain of Others (Same Ethnicity): Does not demonstrate minimum response.

Pain of Others (Different Ethnicity): Does not demonstrate minimum response.

Conclusion: Does not meet the minimum criteria.

Her mum picks up and she tells her everything.

That Þórir is trying to get rid of her and Breki blocked her.

That she's taking medication and failed the test again.

'I feel so used,' says Eyja. 'What do I do?'

Her mum hedges.

Eventually, her mum says that maybe she should look at this as an opportunity. That she should pop in for one of those psychological appointments. She's got nothing to lose.

'Excuse me, there is no reason for *me* to "pop in" with a

psychologist. If there's anyone in this family who needs therapy, it's you.'

Jæja, her mum says after a moment. Her father will be wanting dinner soon, she should probably start cooking.

15.

Óli doesn't put it together when the police send him a picture of the lop-eared boy. It's Sólveig who squints at the photo and asks whether that isn't the boy from the first MASC video, the one who has the brother in jail and is saving up for an apartment. He's thrilled when he sees she's right. He's starting to call Himnar when she gently takes his arm, asks him to think it through for a moment.

'Think about what?'

'Don't take this to the media.'

'Why not?'

'Didn't you see the video? Didn't you hear the kind of life he's had? Of course he's angry.'

'Sólveig,' he says cautiously, 'this boy has been sending us death threats for weeks. He's stalked us. He took pictures of us.' He points to the window as if in corroboration. 'Meanwhile, he's racking up pity points with the nation. Yes, he deserves our compassion, but he's also dangerous. Which is precisely why we need this system. Which is precisely why we need the marking mandate. So that boys like him will get help.'

'They were just empty words. He didn't do anything.'

'He slashed our tyres! All four!'

'C'mon, lay off it. Just stop. I can't deal with you any more.'

'Why am I the bad guy all of a sudden? You've seen the messages. He said he was going to kill us in our sleep.'

'He's angry and desperate and twenty-one years old. He looks at you and sees the face of the man who's ruining his life,' says Sólveig.

'That doesn't justify violence.'

'No, but it explains violence.'

'So we're just supposed to automatically forgive violence because we understand it?'

Sólveig looks at him without looking at him.

'What harm did he actually do to you, Óli? Why blow this up in the media when we know that, by doing so, we'll be putting him in far greater jeopardy than he put us in? Is that justice?'

'What would you have me do? Just let it go?'

'You're the one who's fighting for an empathetic society.'

'This is a trap, Sólveig. We're supposed to feel sorry for him, that's the whole point of the video. But you know as well as I do that all they've got to do is open a window into this boy's world, show what a hard time he's had, and publicly air his plight. And then we the viewers stop thinking about whether he's a danger to his fellow citizens or not, because, suddenly, we have the insight we need to put ourselves in his shoes. Do you think I don't want to save him? Of course, I do. But empathy and compassion are just as blinding as hate or fear or anger or love. Just as blinding as prejudice. Anyone can slap on an expression of suffering. Anyone can tell their

160

sob story. For generation after generation, empathy has been spoon-fed to people as some sort of cure-all, but no generation yet has managed to distinguish empathy from leniency. This is the answer, Sólveig. This is a humane solution. We have the tools to see who needs help. Believe me, it won't do him any good if we look the other way, enable him and hope that our mercy will make him a better person. We can't let ourselves be controlled by our feelings. Sometimes, we need to be cold and think logically about what's best for the whole. That boy is a ticking time bomb.'

'Then offer him psychological treatment.'

'What?'

'If you're so concerned about him, offer him treatment, instead of pressing charges and exposing him in the papers. I'll see him.'

'Sólveig. That's not a fair demand.'

Her expression hardens before she looks away. Then the police call to inform him that a psychologist has determined that the boy doesn't pose any genuine threat to Óli. He won't be held in preventative custody.

Fifty-eight per cent in favour. Magnús Geirsson asks MASC's supporters not to hold any further protests; every time there's a skirmish, support for the mandate goes up. He points to the past two weeks as proof. He asks unmarked people to share the videos instead. With friends, family, co-workers, clubs and social organisations.

Óli gets to the office early on Saturday morning, sits at

a remove in a convex chair over by the window. He finds the video of the boy, projects it before him. The counter in the bottom corner shows how many times it's been viewed: 117,943. Listening to the boy speak, Óli is overwhelmed by the same feeling he gets whenever he listens to the less fortunate. When his mother's hair started going grey, she would sit on a stool on the bathroom floor and ask him to find the silvery strands, to pluck them out one by one. He has the same feeling now, it's almost as if, hidden somewhere on the boy's head, there's a grey hair that's rankling him. And if they could just find that grey hair, just ferret it out and pull it up by the root, all the boy's troubles would vanish in an instant. He could sit back, shut up, and educate himself.

Won't be held in preventative custody.

If he were a woman, the police would be handling this matter differently. There are only two weeks left until the referendum. They're losing support. And Sólveig thinks it is perfectly acceptable that the boy be allowed to spin his tragic tale and work on the hearts and minds of the public – even as he's sending essay-long death threats on the sly. Óli plays the video a third time. He's seen it all before. The isolation and the turmoil. The rage of the victim. Seen how pain and addiction can curtail someone's field of vision, understands how the boy's own interests have become his only reality. The grey hair that can be pulled out by the root.

He leans his head back, closes his eyes. He feels the boy at large in the city, doing his damage. Feels the boy infecting others with his pain. The scope broadens – he feels thousands of bodies moving in the city, bodies that can all claim a piece of this same pain. Óli calls his colleague with the police and asks if Tristan was one of the boys who was arrested during the protests. He holds while his colleague looks the boy up.

'Tristan Máni Axelsson,' says his colleague. 'No criminal record.'

'Wonderful. Thanks.'

Óli stares down at the street below. Someone brings in a bag of pastries. Someone brews coffee. Gradually, the bustle of the office picks up. A single conversation here and there turns into melodious chatter. Even though no one is taking weekends off in the lead-up to the referendum, the atmosphere is more relaxed than usual. Then someone sees a new op-ed in the paper: an economist talking about the financial crisis the opposition never tires of predicting. The team starts fashioning a response.

On Sunday evening, they have dinner at his parents' house. He gets home around seven and they walk over, Dagný in the middle. They swing her between them with forced levity. They haven't mentioned the boy since Friday. Óli is trying to act normal, even though he knows full well that Sólveig can read him like an open book.

Dagný runs straight into her grandma's arms and Sólveig follows them into the living room. Óli goes into the kitchen, where his father is standing at the stove in a blue apron, listening to the news. One of the biggest investment firms in the country made its staff take the test last month and an executive was fired as a result. It's been in the news all week. The executive says he's going to pursue legal action. The newsreader has it from the CEO that the man can't be trusted to fulfil his duties now that his test results have come to light.

'Can't be trusted,' his father mutters and throws up his hands, a wooden spoon in one and a fork in the other. He looks at Óli. 'Tell me, what's become of trusting your people? Are we just giving up on trust as a concept now?'

Óli leans his head on the wall behind him.

'The entire situation is about trust,' says his mother perfunctorily as she walks into the kitchen. 'It's about being able to trust people.'

'But this isn't trust!' says his father. 'Trust is by its nature uncertainty. Trust is about believing people, not about being sure. Being sure is being sure.'

It's not out of character for his father to suddenly be concerned with trusting others, even though he often argues for stricter border controls, and favours the death penalty when it suits him.

'When we talk about trustworthy objects, a part of that is about being sure,' says Óli. 'A trustworthy bridge is a bridge you can be sure of.'

'Yes, but when we talk about people, the meaning changes,' answers his father, giving the pan a rough shake. 'People aren't bridges. People are planks with different load-bearing capacities.'

None of them had anything to add to that.

—

Óli feels like he can't take in any more information. He is a cup that's been filled to the brim, sloshing over at the slightest touch. His body constantly aches from fatigue. He jumps when he looks in the mirror. He wakes on Tuesday with a sore jaw and knows he's been grinding his teeth at night. Zoé says he got eleven minutes of deep sleep. At the end-of-day meeting, he's asked to answer questions from the press. He knows he should say yes. But he can't. He looks from face to face and says he can't do it today. He's got to go home and rest. He comes home to an empty house, falls asleep as soon as he lies down in the living room. He stirs when his wife and daughter come home but stays sprawled on the sofa. Dagný runs in and hops up onto his belly, laughing as she bounces, and he pulls her down to him, holds her tight, hoping she'll let him hug her for a moment, but she wriggles with laughter until he lets go.

Sólveig is in the kitchen putting away groceries. Dagný hears the bags rustling and rushes over, doubtless to extract some treat that was bought at the store. He gets to his feet. With difficulty.

'I'll offer him therapy.'

Sólveig looks up from the bags.

'Really?'

'Yes.'

She sighs happily. Strides across the kitchen and lays her head on his chest. When she puts her arms around him, something inside him goes slack, loosens after having been stretched taut for a long time.

16.

The cops finally let Tristan go once they've traced the messages and he's admitted he wrote them. He can't stop fucking shaking. It's a good thing he kept his mouth shut. He was about to tell them where the car with all the shit from the apartment building in Kópavogur was parked when the bald cop started talking about Ólafur Tandri and the messages Tristan sent. He just looked at the bald cop and said, Huh? and then the cop with the hair said that Ólafur Tandri had Chaperone Plus, ergo they were watching his house. Wasn't that fucking illegal, he asked the cop with the hair, recording people who are just out for a walk in their neighbourhood, and then the bald cop said it isn't illegal if there's a crime in question.

'Crime? What crime?' asked Tristan.

The cop with the hair said it was a crime to send 'that kind of message' and if Ólafur Tandri decided to press charges, that it could mean a *considerable* fine and when he asked the cop with the hair how *considerable*, he wouldn't give an estimate. Tristan asked over and over how much he thought it might be and tried to guess the number and all the bald cop would say was, You'll just have to wait and see. Then when Tristan asked how much longer they would keep him there, the cop with the hair said they were going to let the psychologist decide if they should keep him in preventative custody.

'Preventative custody??' Tristan said.

'That means you'd be held here for a few days, if the pyschologist determines that you're *hættulegur*.'

'*Hættulegur*??'

'Yeah, shall I say it in English for you? Dangerous. If the psychologist determines that you're dangerous.'

'I know what hættulegur means!'

'Good. I thought maybe we'd need to get a translator in here.'

'A translator?'

'Sometimes we need to get a translator.'

'For what?'

'To explain the big Icelandic words. I'm terrible at explaining big words.'

'I don't need a fucking translator! I'm Icelandic!'

'Alright, tiger,' he said. Then the psychologist came in, freckled and brown-haired and so pretty and she gave Tristan such a nice look that he just stared at the table. She said her name was Dröfn and asked if he might consider taking the empathy test. If he took it, he probably wouldn't be taken into custody.

He explained as well as he could that No, he could not consider taking the test, that was not an option. If he took the test, he'd be betraying everything he believed in, himself and his brother and all his friends. He would never do any of the stuff he wrote in those messages. He'd seen Ólafur Tandri

168

going into his house three months ago and that's when he started writing all that shit, shit he'd never actually do, it just made him feel a little better, it was, like, a release for all intensive purposes, because Ólafur Tandri was always popping up in those ads, every single fucking day, he couldn't open Zoé without hearing that guy's fucking voice telling him to 'pop in' or 'think about the future'.

Dröfn gave him a friendly smile and so he just kept going and said he never started shit, þú veist, never threw the first punch, not even when Rúrik tried to get him to, because his brother was always starting shit with other guys to get some street cred, but he couldn't stand fighting, it was fucking terrible, so he'd never start shit with the PSYCH guy for reals. But he had slashed those tyres and would pay for them. He'd just been so mad. But he would never do anything like really, actually bad.

'I believe you, Tristan,' said Dröfn. 'I saw you in that video the other day. I'm going to say you can be trusted. But you have to promise me you won't go anywhere near Ólafur Tandri or his family again. From now on, you're going to have to take the long way home so you don't pass his house. Ólafur Tandri has everything he needs to see you convicted.'

'I swear,' said Tristan and she was being so nice that in that moment he practically exploded he was so thankful, and he's still fucking dying from how thankful he is as he walks back to his neighbourhood. His teeth are chattering and he's still shaking deep in his fucking bones but he is so dead-arse fucking thankful.

He calls Eldór when he gets home and tells him what happened. Eldór's face fills the screen and Tristan can see glass behind him, which means Eldór is out on his balcony.

'Fuck. Do you think they got a warrant to look at the grams we've sent each other? My probation, man.'

'No, just the ones I sent the PSYCH guy.'

'Okay, okay,' says Eldór. 'I just got back from the countryside, the car's where it should be. Viktor said the container would go on Thursday. We'll get paid for it the week after next.'

'Two weeks! I'm never going to fucking make it.'

'Why not?'

'Because the vote is next Saturday. That means I only have a few days to buy an apartment if the money from Viktor is enough and I'll also have to pay some fucking fine if the PSYCH guy decides to press charges because I sent those messages.'

'Wait up, why do you for sure have to buy a place before the vote? You know it'll take some time before we actually have to take the test, even if the marking law passes.'

'Yeah, but if the marking law passes, they can make me take the test before I can buy an apartment or get a loan or whatever the fuck, you get it? I won't be able to say no any more.'

Eldór stares just above the camera while he thinks.

'Maybe you should just take the test.'

'What? Nei. What's wrong with you?'

'Yeah, dude, it fucking sucks, I get it. But just . . . maybe you'll pass it. Then you could get a loan and buy that basement apartment.'

'Street-level.'

'Tristan, sorry, man, but you gotta save yourself, dude. You could go to the bank tomorrow and take their test without having to mark yourself or anything. Just saying. I would if I were you.'

He calls his dad and asks if there's any chance he could front him and his dad says no. He calls Sölvi and Sölvi says no, too. They both think he wants money for trex, even though he tells them over and over why he needs the money. He thinks about calling Magnús Geirsson and looks up his number, but chickens out just before he's about to make the call.

An actual human being calls him from the bank. Tristan tries to explain the situation, and the service rep nods into the camera, but says that there's really nothing he can do, although Tristan could try to make a lower offer on the apartment.

'Okay, já. Can we give that a try?'

'Of course,' says the service rep and then he suggests a price, based on what Tristan has in savings and whatever fees. 'If this offer is rejected, then you just keep going, offer this amount for any of the available flats you find.'

'Right,' says Tristan. 'Thanks. For reals.'

But he's still really fucking stressed when he's getting ready to call the agent so he takes more trex than usual, which is really fucking stupid because he needs to be saving money, but he can't take the backflips he feels inside him when he thinks about what the cop said, that Ólafur Tandri could press charges and he might have to go to jail or pay him tons of money. He calls and as calmly and politely as he can says that he wants to make an offer on the apartment.

'Offer on the apartment, yeah,' says the agent.

'That's right.'

'Wonderful. I'm sending you the purchase offer form now. Fill it out and then send it back to me.'

Tristan's watch pings when he receives the form. He projects it onto the kitchen table, fills it out with his finger, and sends it straight back. Then he gets some frozen shit from the freezer and heats it up and eats like he hasn't eaten in months.

He lies on the mattress in his bedroom playing CityScrapers and doesn't pick up when his mum calls. Then he gets a message. It's from Sunneva. She asks what he's doing. He sits up. It's the first time in three months she's messaged him. It's twelve-thirty, she must be wondering if she can come over. He says he's just hanging out at home and asks where she's at. He waits and waits for an answer and imagines that she's drunk at some party and there are some fucking sick dudes trying to take advantage of her and that he's going to go save her and get her home and put her in bed and spread a blanket over her like in the movies and then she'll wake up tomorrow and be so thankful and want to be his girlfriend.

'You should come over if you want,' he adds. He stares at

her name and waits. Then, after a few minutes, he lies back down on the mattress and tries to forget that she sent anything and goes back to playing CityScrapers.

If Viktor hadn't been such a fucking bastard, he and Sunneva might be boyfriend and girlfriend today. He met her at a party that one of his old friends from high school threw. He'd been so happy when he was invited. Those guys didn't talk to him for six months after he fucked things up by stealing from one of them, so he put on nice clothes and did his hair (this was before he shaved his head) and even though he'd been saving like a motherfucker, he stopped at an ATM on the way and took out money. All his old friends were in the kitchen when he got there and he went straight over to them and said Hi, and they said hi, too, everyone but the friend Tristan stole from, he didn't say anything, and then he just stood there and listened to his old friends talk, and laughed when they laughed, and then at some point the friend who'd invited him said in front of everyone that he was glad to see him, man, and the others said they were, too.

Ergo Tristan told them about his job down at the harbour and that he was trying to get his addiction under control (which was maybe not a hundred per cent true but still he *wanted* to quit), and he felt fucking terrible about what happened and then he looked at the friend he stole from and said, Sorry, that I stole from you, Örvar, and then he looked at the rest of them and said, Sorry it took me so long to pay you all back, and then he pulled the money out of his pocket and the guys said Neeei, nah, man, it's cool, but he said,

Really, it will make *me* feel better, and they let him pay them back and then they all raised their glasses: *Skál*. After that, he felt so much fucking lighter and when he met Sunneva later on, he was so goddamn happy and couldn't stop smiling. He was the best version of himself and could just talk to her like a normal person.

They laughed and talked for an insanely long time about all sorts of shit until everyone decided to go downtown and then Sunneva asked if he was going to go, too, and he said, Nah, I'm not marked, and then she said, Hey, me neither! and laughed such a pretty laugh and then she asked if he wanted to go to her place and he didn't understand what was happening when they started walking together through the snow, what fucking guardian angels were watching over him that night.

A week later, they hung out and just drove around the city together, they got ice cream and went back to her place (or her parents' place, but she lived in the basement, which had its own toilet and everything) and Tristan remembered thinking, when he walked home the next day, that maybe, if he were as nice to her as he could possibly be, that then things would stay like this, that maybe he could see her every weekend until maybe he'd get to see her more often and then maybe they could be boyfriend and girlfriend and he could sleep next to her every night and wake up with her every day.

He was at work and sending her a gram when the customs guy showed up literally out of nowhere and asked to see the container that he was a hundred per cent not supposed to fucking see, and then the cops did a whole investigation. No

174

one got busted, thank Christ, but Viktor blamed Tristan for everything even though Tristan had done EXACTLY what he was supposed to do, he'd gone and found the customs guy at the right time and then let everyone know when Fart Juice had inspected a normal container. How was he supposed to know the customs guy would come back? That never happened. Just out of nowhere he came down a second time and pointed at the container from the countryside, which of course was full of stolen shit and not the Genuine Icelandic Handcrafts it was supposed to be full of. There was nothing Tristan could have done and he didn't fucking do anything wrong. But Viktor wouldn't look at him and said that it was Tristan who had to answer to all the guys who wanted their money for that fucking container. Tristan had seen those guys, and those guys were much, much worse addicts than he was, so he just said Okay, what do I do? and Viktor said You're just going to have to fill a new container, I'll give you two weeks. Two weeks. It was literally fucking impossible and Viktor knew it. These containers were jam-packed with furniture and motorcycles and car parts – filling one container was a two-week hunting expedition for like twenty guys, maybe. Ergo, Tristan took two weeks off so he could clean house after fucking house and that was actually when his stomach pain got bad for reals and the knot turned into a feeling like he was being stabbed and he got a stinging in his chest and stopped being able to take deep breaths. And after two weeks of that hell, he had of course only filled like half a container and Viktor said Tristan would just have to pay the difference because otherwise, he'd tell all those guys who'd really fucked the whole thing up and Tristan didn't have the guts to do anything but transfer the money to Viktor. It was literally like three months' pay, money that Tristan couldn't afford to lose if he was ever going to buy an apartment. And that was when he figured out that he needed to get the fuck out of this job. He couldn't risk having to do that ever again.

But the worst thing was that while he was dealing with all this crazy shit, he made the insanely stupid mistake of not talking to Sunneva. He just couldn't be relaxed or fun – any time she sent something he tried to answer, but everything he wrote or recorded sounded so fucking fake and forced because he felt so terrible, so he just sent back one or two-word answers. And then, when he'd finally paid Viktor for half the container and given himself a few days to feel better from all the stomach pain, he sent her a message and said Sorry I haven't been around the last three weeks. I just had so much shit going on. Did she want to meet up? Then two days passed and she didn't answer and he said sorry again and that he'd been a total idiot but he really was so into her.

Then she answered: Fool me once, shame on you. Fool me twice, shame on me, and it didn't matter what Tristan wrote or sent her after that, she never answered. She sent him one gram in January, at two in the morning, super drunk and way too close to the camera, asking where he was, but he didn't see it until the next day and then he did his hair and put on a collared shirt and spent a stupid amount of time arranging the camera and sending her a gram where he said he was like, crazy happy to get the gram from her and then he asked if she wanted to meet up that week but he never heard back.

One hour passes and then two. Sunneva doesn't answer. But then someone calls and he springs up in bed.

His mum. He mutes it.

When he wakes up later on the mattress, he's still in all his clothes and has his headphones in and watch on. Sunneva hasn't answered but his mum has called a few times in a row and sent him a gram where she says she has to talk to him and she's so fucking hysterical that Tristan gets worried that maybe something happened. To Rúrik maybe, or his sister. So he calls her back.

At first, he can't hear anything she's saying. She's just screaming words like 'unbelievable,' 'can't believe,' 'what will,' 'and Rúrik,' and then she screams some more and Tristan has to wait until he can finally talk.

'What do you think Rúrik is going to say? And what do you think your dad's going to say? And what do you think Sölvi will do when he sees it? I can't believe you, Tristan. I can't believe you did this.'

'Did what?'

'You made me sound like a monster! What do you think people are going to say?'

'What the fuck are you talking about?'

'The video, Tristan! That horrible video!'

'Oh, yeah that.'

'*Yeah, that!*'

'I had to do it. I needed the money.'

'I don't believe it. I can't believe you.'

'What was I supposed to fucking do? I've got to buy an apartment before the vote. I can't live with you.'

'Of course you can live with me and you know it!'

'Nei. I'm not welcome where you live.'

'Tristan,' she says. 'Please. Just take the test. It's just one little test, you've got nothing to lose. There's a bedroom here for you. Your sister misses you. She looks up to you so much. She listens to you. I can't do this alone.'

'No! I've told you a million fucking times! It was you who decided this, not me.'

'Where did you boys get this stubbornness? I'm not this stubborn. You father isn't this stubborn. You're just like bulls, the pair of you.'

She sighs dramatically.

'You've got to talk to your brother,' says his mum. 'Rúrik is going to lose his mind when he finds out you talked about him publicly.'

'Já, já.'

'I mean it, Tristan.'

'I said yeah! I already know he's going to be mad!'

'I'm not going to be a go-between. You can't call me to smooth things over.'

'I gotta go.'

'Tristan—'

'I'll talk to you later,' he says. 'Bye.'

—

The agent calls him on Monday and says his offer has been rejected. He's sending back a counter-offer.

The counter-offer is too high. He can see that right off. He rejects the counter-offer and asks Zoé to look for apartments at the price that the service rep said he could manage. Zoé says there are no apartments in the capital area listed at that price, but here are the cheapest ones. There are five, and two of those are on marked floors. All the same price as the street-level apartment he wants to buy, but all of them are basements, studios, twenty-five to thirty-two square metres. He asks Zoé to make an appointment to see the ones that are unmarked.

He finds Viktor at work and asks if he can come in after lunch the next day. Viktor says yes but that he owes him. He doesn't say anything about seeing the MASC video where Tristan said he was looking for a new job. Maybe he doesn't think it's that big a deal.

Tristan's sweating and paranoid when he drives out of the underground garage and stops to get more trex. He waits until he relaxes, until his body goes loose. Then he projects the mask and rings the bells at an old apartment building in the suburbs until someone lets him in. The first apartments have major security systems, so he moves on to the apartment one floor down, which doesn't have anything – no ultra-locks and no stickers.

Then he lugs all his shit down to the car, drives to a new garage, tells Eldór, and takes the S to work. Why haven't the cops called him? Eldór and Wojciech are in D2 so he goes to D1 and works across from Oddur and tries not to think about the fucking fine and how much it will be if Ólafur Tandri decides to press charges.

'Good day, my homies, guess what happened this week, já, this happened – an unmarked man was shot five times in the head by cops in the US. What was he doing? He was getting his driver's licence from his car. That's what's going to happen here if we're not careful, all the cops have to do is get a picture of your face, run it through their database, and if you're unmarked they're immediately fourteen times more scared for their lives and fourteen times more likely to shoot you. Is this what we want? NEI. We have to fight for basic human rights. We have to fight so the powers that be don't start sorting us into first and second class. The lives of marked people aren't more important than our lives. We were born on this planet. We have just as much right to freedom as other people, just as much right to trust, free of charge. But no, in their system, we have to work for it. We have to smile and bow and humble ourselves all the time, be super polite all the time, even if we're having an off day. Because if we don't bend the knee, then we're dangerous.'

His stomach is killing him. Why isn't the fucking trex kicking in? He's taken two today, that's more than he's supposed to take. He works until five o'clock and has just decided to walk home, so he won't have to go by Ólafur Tandri's house, when he gets a call from an unknown number.

'Halló?'

'Yes, is this Tristan Máni?'

'Uh huh.'

'Good evening. This is Ólafur Tandri.'

Tristan stops in the middle of the street.

'Are you there?'

'Yes.'

'Great. Listen, I've had a few days to think it over, and I've decided not to press charges for the threats.'

'Are you serious?'

'Yes. If you agree to attend ten therapy appointments and take the empathy test.'

'Not a fucking chance.'

'You don't have to mark yourself. You don't have to do anything but show up. The appointments are free. The test is just so the psychologist can assess your situation.'

'I'd rather pay a fine than take that fucking test.'

'Tristan,' says Ólafur Tandri, 'I've met a hundred boys your age and I've a knack for seeing who's going to pass and who isn't. You'll pass. No question. This doesn't have to be so hard.'

Tristan looks at the apartment building nearest him. The blinds in the partly mirrored windows are these, like, trendy kind of hanging blinds made up of all these different shapes.

'Tristan?'

'I . . . nei! This isn't fucking fair.'

'It will help you. I promise.'

'Why can't all of you just leave me alone? Why can't I just have some peace?'

'Because you live in a society with other people. That's the sacrifice we all make in order to reap the benefits.'

'But what if I don't want to live in a society? Where the fuck can I go?'

'Tristan,' says Ólafur Tandri, and he's way too fucking calm, like Tristan is stupid or something. 'People have said all kinds of things about the mark and the Registry. That the government is monitoring people's results and that police are forcing people to take the test against their will. That's not true. The test is to help people better understand themselves. You wouldn't be sending these kinds of messages if you didn't feel bad. If you fail the test, which I know isn't going to happen, then we will help you pass. You can buy an apartment and go back to school and lead a normal life.'

'Tell that to my fucking brother. He went into psychological treatment and the only thing that happened was that he turned into a fucking junkie. And me, too.'

'I completely understand that you're angry,' says Ólafur Tandri. 'I would be, too, in your shoes. But some would say that addiction is just a symptom of the problem, not the root. That a person with substance abuse issues needs to consider whether there's some other, more serious problem underlying the addiction. The first step is to talk with a psychologist and have the space to lay all your cards on the table, everything that's troubling you. Then, together, you can start to determine what the main issue is. It could be a past trauma or a poor self-image or difficulty connecting with the people closest to you. Your friends and family.'

Tristan listens. He thinks about his mum and his sister and the extra bedroom at their house that's just for him. Then he thinks about Rúrik.

'You don't have to answer right away,' says Ólafur Tandri. 'Take a few days to think it over. You could just take the test and see the psychologist and, after ten sessions, move on with your life.' Ólafur Tandri waits for a second, but when Tristan doesn't say anything, he keeps going: 'You'll think it over?'

'Okay. Alright.'

'Good deal. Just give me a call in the next few days.'

17.

Alexandria doesn't know which way is up: she's relieved, she's mad, she's lost whole chunks of hair in the past month, she gets more and more depressed about the tufts left behind in her brush – she should stop brushing, it just doesn't work any more – but when she doesn't brush, her hair gets so gross, she's frazzled, she doesn't hear a word people say to her because she's so distracted by the matted tangles in her hair, which gets flatter and more unmanageable by the day, like roughly felted wool. She's been waking up multiple times a night for a month, gasping awake like she's overslept, two-something in the morning, three-something, four-something, five-something; Naómí looks at her with such disgust and contempt, doesn't have the slightest idea that her expressions push all of Alexandria's buttons, that her mother's self-confidence is the size of an insect right now, and no matter how soft a voice Alexandria uses, or how well she cocoons the two of them, even if she cooks a nice dinner and makes everything perfect so they can have a cosy movie night, spend some time together, her daughter would still rather lock herself in her bedroom, not see her mother, not hug her, not talk to her, listen to her or look at her. Sometimes, she wants to scream at Naómí to give her a fucking break, to tell her everything that's happened in her life, everything she's done to make them safe, but she knows she can't put all that on her fourteen-year-old daughter, so she says nothing, just yells at her inside her head while she stares at the floor and waits for her daughter to get older, more mature, waits for her adolescence to pass, and hopefully, her contempt as well. And on top of the anxiety and the stress and the hair loss, she's also had such pangs of dread since she went to the school to talk to that teacher, she shouldn't have done that, like it wasn't enough that she'd bared her soul to the headmistress, in confidence, and now she doesn't know if the teacher will treat that conversation as private or not, because of course she forgot to ask her not to say anything to anyone else, she forgot Rule Number One – *always ask them not to tell* – because if you don't, you only have yourself to blame if your private business gets out, that's something you learn on a small island, and even more so in a small town on a small island. Alexandria used to treat all her personal information like dogs on leashes, she never blurted anything out, never, not after Karen Lind (who was supposed to have been her best friend) told everyone who she lost her virginity to in the first semester of sixth form, gossip that she probably could have handled if the boy had *known* it was her first time, which wasn't what happened; actually, she'd teased him when he hesitated, as if to shift the focus away from herself, she'd acted like she'd known the ropes. Since then, she'd always kept her business to herself, but it was like a dam burst after her relationship with Sölvi, she's got no stopper any more, no filters and no stopper, as soon as anyone gives her silence, she fills it with words, shifts into high gear and then spends the next however many weeks patching herself back up at home. The teacher didn't need to know that she'd failed, the teacher didn't need to know that Sölvi couldn't get into the neighbourhood, but Alexandria was so anxious about the idea of having to move again, she'd started losing so much hair, that she needed some sort of reassurance, and the headmistress actually frightened her, she'd hoped that the form teacher would be more welcoming and understanding, but that wasn't at all the case, the woman's eyes hardened the minute she'd blurted out that she'd failed; she'd watched her smile stiffen and her long neck, too. And after all that, now that the wait is finally over, now that they've finally got the email saying Naómí passed, and better days are on the horizon, what does she see while she's looking at clothes online? Out of nowhere, a video of Tristan pops up, he's telling the whole country about their home life, about her and Sölvi and Rúrik, and he does such a bad job of answering those horrible, confusing questions that people are going to read something much worse between the lines, they'll think that *she* is the source of all the problems, that the boys misbehaved because *she* neglected them, that it was *her* fault that Rúrik turned out the way he turned out – because she made him go to a psychologist and made him go on meds, which weren't so great after all, but how on earth was she supposed to know that, she wasn't psychic, she couldn't see the future, she was told that trex would create the happy hormones that the brain makes when you feel love or closeness with other people and that these hormones would have a positive effect on his nervous system. How was she supposed to know that it would be so addictive, that trex would be labelled a narcotic within just a couple of years? The doctors told her it was good for her kid and she listened to them, and, for a while, Rúrik was doing better, a lot better even, he scored a lot higher on the test after he'd been taking trex for a year, but that was back when he had a good psychologist and it was also the year that Sölvi had a good job that he liked and that paid well, which meant they argued a lot less about money and she didn't go out and buy stuff as often to make herself feel better. Sölvi didn't go crazy every time she came home from the shops, didn't immediately fish the receipt out of her bags and ask what she was thinking buying such expensive jam, or a whole chicken, even though it was Friday and they hadn't eaten a decent meal all week, just spaghetti with ham and spaghetti with hot dogs and frozen pizzas and cheese sandwiches and when Sölvi got really stressed out about money, he'd even get upset when she bought milk for the cereal, because he said it made no difference if you put milk or water in cereal, and in those moments, all she could do was yell that he could put water in his own fucking cereal but no child of hers was ever going to do that. But that year, they didn't have those arguments, that year was a good year, that was the year that Sölvi got a good salary and liked his job and Rúrik, who was probably sixteen at the time, started to unclench, and she started to unclench, too, and that was the year she passed the test the first time, after failing it four years earlier and losing her job with the city, which she knows now was because she was in emotional shutdown from living with Sölvi. It took her a long time to realise that she wasn't a bad person, that her brain was protecting itself because even though Sölvi never beat her after that one time, she could still never relax around him, her body couldn't trust him after that evening she went out for a girls' night with her friends and promised to come home before midnight – she'd pumped and pumped all that day so that Sölvi could feed Naómí if she woke up. They'd started feeding Naómí porridge around that time and it sometimes gave her a tummy ache, and then she'd cry late into the night, which is, of course, what happened the evening she got caught up in the moment at the bar and her phone died – this was back before everyone could afford a holosystem like Zoé. She remembered scream-singing with her friends on the dance floor and going to the bar, where an older man bought drinks for her and her friends. Alexandria felt like the man was talking to her the most and she liked it, she'd never felt as ugly as she did that first year breastfeeding Naómí, and her stomach didn't seem to be going back the way it did when she had the boys, so she drank in the man's attention, she laughed and smiled and then, all of a sudden, there was Sölvi, just off to the side behind the man, and she was so shocked that she just grabbed her coat and followed him out without saying goodbye, and when she asked who was at home looking after the kids, he said the boys were home with Naómí – the boys, who were eight and eleven years old – she asked what he was thinking, driving all the way downtown from Fossvogur and leaving an eight- and eleven-year-old by themselves with a seven-month-old baby, was he as stupid as he looked, had he lost his mind, and that was when he made a U-turn and drove into a car park. She asked what the hell he was doing when he threw himself out of the car, even though her body knew exactly what he was going to do before he yanked open her door, dragged her out, and began raining down blows upon her, blows her body never forgot, not for one second of the next twelve years, even though Sölvi kept the promise he made three days later, when he came home shaking, his best friend in tow, and said he'd never do it again. But nei, her body never forgot, and it jumped every time Sölvi made a sudden move and so Sölvi never forgot either, and he resented her for that, he hated her for reminding him of what he'd done and then he started doing what Tristan talked about in that awful interview (how could he do that to her), started forming a little boys' team against her. Everything she did was hysteria, was stupid and laughable, and when Sölvi made fun of her, the boys would join in, and she went numb, she started buying stuff to feel better and eating to feel better, and that made Sölvi crazy because they were sinking deeper into debt with every year, and Sölvi scolded her every single day and took every opportunity to belittle her in front of the boys, which triggered her flight when really she needed to fight, those times when she forbade the boys from hanging around the neighbourhood after ten or made them study for a test, that's when she'd stand her ground, like she was nailed there, and yell at them, it was the only thing they took seriously, it was the only line they didn't cross, up until Sölvi lost his good job and Rúrik got hooked on trex and dropped out of school without telling them, started selling trex so he'd have money for trex, and Tristan tried as hard as he could to copy his big brother, who was just like their dad, while Tristan was more like her, he was more sensitive and easy-going. Which is why it was so important to her that Rúrik got some mental balance, because she knew if the older brother's life was a mess, the younger would follow right behind him, but nothing came of it, Rúrik just got madder and madder with every year, and even though she felt like the world was ending when he moved out just before he turned eighteen, it also relieved a lot of pressure at home, and even though the world ended a second time when he was arrested with trex, it was also a good thing, when you thought about it, because he'd get a good psychologist and new medication that would help him get off the trex so that maybe he'd be better when he came back from serving his sentence next year, who knows, maybe he'd even pass the test finally, and then maybe Tristan would stop with all this ridiculous stubbornness, which a hundred per cent only cropped up because of Rúrik, it's like Tristan thinks that taking the test is selling out his brother, that he can't leave him behind all by himself, just like Tristan feels like she betrayed him by moving here to the marked neighbourhood even though she begged him to take the test and come with them when they had to run away from Sölvi.

But if the marking law passes, Tristan will be forced to take the test and will see that he's normal, of course he's normal, and when he does, he'll come back to her, she didn't go back and forth between contractors for no reason, she wouldn't accept fewer than three bedrooms, she couldn't care less about the view or the noise or if it was inconvenient, the only things she insisted on were that it had to be an apartment in this neighbourhood and it had to have three bedrooms, they could be stamp-sized for all she cared. And if Rúrik passed the test next year and wanted to move home, she'd sleep in the living room, she's waited and waited to find a free sleeper sofa on the internet, just to leave open the possibility that she'll have all her children back with her. Maybe the boys could finish sixth form like normal people and maybe they could go to university or technical college and leave the past behind, start over. But now, Naómí will see that video and Alexandria knows without a shadow of a doubt that it's going to make her act out, hearing such a fragmented version of their life, even though Naómí knows perfectly well how things were and why they moved into the marked neighbourhood, why Alexandria changed the locks the day after the policewoman came to their house and told her what Sölvi had done to the poor woman he'd been seeing for ages and that he'd been charged with attempted murder, and she just looked at the policewoman's lips and felt like all her words were hand grenades on the kitchen table and someone had taken the pins out, and then they exploded and the shock wave that followed slammed into her chest and went all through her body, organ by organ, through her heart and lungs and stomach, and after the policewoman left, she felt like her eyes had been replaced with camera lenses, and she felt that way for many weeks afterwards, when Sölvi was sentenced to eighteen months in jail, too, she felt like none of this had anything to do with her, not really, it had nothing to do with her life, and when she filed for divorce and custody, the social worker said it would help if she marked herself and then she failed, of course. The social worker looked for ways to help her and her psychologist Gréta explained that nearly everything that had gone wrong in her life had happened in response to violence, violence that could be traced to her children's fathers, and her choice of partners could be traced to her parents, and for the next month, she felt like a volcano that was awakening after centuries and might explode at any moment, and she had crying fits and rage fits and depression fits, and she started writing down when she overate and overbought and how she'd been feeling right before and, slowly but surely, she started having feelings for her children again, love and guilt and shame, feelings that were buried under all this wreckage, and at some point Gréta asked if she wanted to take the empathy test again, to measure her progress, and then she passed, she scored just over the minimum, and Gréta said this was just the beginning, that now the main work was to ensure her continued mental stability, and as soon as the divorce went through, she sold the apartment and her half was just enough for a down payment on an apartment here in the marked neighbourhood, and the day she moved, she felt like she was finally starting to live the life she wanted to live. Her new life. But life isn't like that, life doesn't just stop rolling along when everything is going well, there's no such thing as a 'triumph over mental illness', all you can do is triumph over each day, one by one, and everything else is an eternal battle, like doing the dishes and all that stuff, but she didn't know that then, and when the high of buying the new apartment wore off, she started longing to buy and eat again, and when they released Sölvi from jail, he charged her with custody interference and his lawyer made her out to be a criminal, suddenly she was the violent one, not the one who was protecting her child from violence, but the judge, thank God, told Sölvi that if he intended to seek custody of Naómí, he'd need to undergo a psychological assessment and take the test, which he categorically refused to do, he wouldn't hear of it. He said he wasn't going to let anyone mess around in his brain, he'd never harmed his daughter and he never would, but Alexandria, on the other hand, she was an unfit mother, his child would be permanently damaged if he didn't gain custody, all the judge needed to do was look at his stepsons, who were both junkies. Alexandria, he said, could not fulfil the fundamental requirements of being a parent, she couldn't maintain a household or get the child to school on time or help her with her homework, and the judge didn't say anything and then several long days passed and then, thank God, he ruled in her favour, but Tristan still wouldn't talk to her and Naómí wouldn't talk to her and she felt Gréta's disapproval because she'd relapsed after all the stress with the custody battle. Gréta judged her because she wasn't constantly improving herself and moving forward, and it wasn't long after that that she started forgetting to write down when she bought something or ate to feel better and then she started feeling anxious about seeing Gréta because Gréta saw through that, and then one day, Gréta scolded her for giving up on herself, like she was a small child and not fifty-one years old, and Alexandria walked out and never went back because she wasn't going to let herself be treated like that. Since then, she's been terrified of failing again, of not passing the test the next time she has to take it, which is five months from now, because here in this neighbourhood, you have to take the test every year, it's not enough to take it once and then be safe for ever. But, fortunately, Naómí passed it, so they have at least five more months, and she knows, a hundred per cent, that she needs to go back to therapy, that this just won't do any longer, but every time she goes to look for a new psychologist, she gets paralysed, it's hanging over her head like a blown-out ceiling light; she knows she needs to buy a new bulb but can't bring herself to do it, she just sits in the dark as if hoping, deep down, that someone else will do it for her, will knock on the door holding a box of lightbulbs, and she'll be so surprised and happy and thankful, and her saviour will grab a stool from the breakfast nook and change the bulb and, all of a sudden, the light will pour over her, the glare in her eyes, and she'll look around the bright room and think to herself: That wasn't so hard, I could have done that myself ages ago.

18.

Daníel is no longer under surveillance.

'Why not?' asks Vetur. 'It's only been ten months since I took out the restraining order. I was told he'd be under surveillance for a year. A year is twelve months.'

'It says here that he underwent a psychological evaluation four months ago,' says her legal advocate, 'after agreeing to undergo treatment. A specialist determined that he's unlikely to offend again. The restraining order still stands, but he's not being monitored by Spotter. He's not permitted to be within two hundred metres of you or to contact you in any way.'

'But he was within two hundred metres of me.'

'I understand. Did he try to make contact with you?'

'No.'

'Did he seem to be following you?'

'No.'

'Okay. It was probably just a coincidence, then. It's a small town, of course, these things can happen. But we'll be in touch with him.'

She's back to square one. She calls in sick. Every day, she feels like Daníel is standing under her bedroom window, every rustle is a footstep, every time she hears a car, she has to peek into the car park from behind the curtains. She starts envying people who own guns, she, who's been anti-gun her whole life, she talks to one friend after another, to her parents; her mum brings her a hot meal every night, rubs her back every night, but as soon as her mum leaves, she has to make two circuits to the window, the front door and the balcony door, then she takes a pill for her anxiety and sleeps in the living room where she's made up a bed on the sofa.

'I've got to move,' she says. 'I can't live here any longer. I can't be pissing myself with terror every day, in my own home. I'm a scamp! A mischief-maker! I'm devil-may-care!'

'I know this is hard,' says her psychologist. 'But he hasn't contacted you for months. It was almost certainly just a chance encounter. And now we also know that he doesn't have a serious moral disorder. This is good news.'

'That doesn't excuse what he did!'

'Absolutely not. But before, we thought it wouldn't be possible to have a conversation with him. Now there's a much better chance.'

'*Have a conversation with him?* You want me to *have a conversation with him?*'

'That's entirely up to you. Other psychologists would likely advise it. He's clearly sought help. Maybe it would be good for you to see how he's improved, maybe it would help you get some closure. He doesn't have a moral disorder, at any rate. He passed the test.'

'I couldn't give a shit if he passed the test! I haven't had a decent night's sleep in over a year!'

'Okay, then you have two options: either you keep working at the Quarter School or you move to a place where you feel more mentally and physically secure.'

'But if I move, I'll feel like I've lost,' says Vetur, 'and he's won.'

'Not at all. You're not responsible for the fact that he's threatening you. You're simply taking appropriate steps to ensure your safety. And if that means you need to move, then you do it. Of your own volition.'

Vetur sinks down in her seat. 'I can't.'

'Yes, you can,' says her psychologist. 'I have every faith in you. Try looking around, considering other opportunities. Wasn't the teaching gig just a temporary job, or what did you call it?'

'An intermission.'

'Exactly. Didn't you want to be an ethicist?'

'Yes, I want to be an ethicist and be on committees and give professional opinions and all that. But I'm not sure of anything any more.'

Her dad gives her a ride to work. When she checks her mailbox, she sees that the Registry has been posted in the school portal. She scans her class list. They all passed. She leans back in her chair. Some part of her had decided that Naómí was going to fail.

She has Year Seven first. The kids trickle in and bunch together and there's a visible release of tension when one of them says, 'God, I was so stressed out,' and another one says,

'No kidding,' and giggles flare up in the classroom, not like a single spark from a flint struck on a desert island, but the sudden burst when lighter fluid is poured on a grill and for a second, everything's aflame and then it dies down again as quickly as it started. Vetur keeps getting tongue-tied in front of the kids, she loses her train of thought over and over again, then one of them points it out and they all laugh and she tries to laugh along with them. The next class is a bit better than the first one and the third a little better than the second, and then finally, when she's locking the classroom door, someone behind her says Hi and she turns around and of course, it's Naómí's mum.

'Good afternoon,' says Vetur.

Alexandria has clearly taken some trouble with herself today; she's wearing make-up and tried to comb her fine hair into a bun; her hands are clasped in front of her, like she's here to ask for something.

'I'm sorry, I know I should have let you know I was coming. Could I have a word with you?'

'Yes,' says Vetur, and unlocks her classroom again, holding the door open as Alexandria walks in.

'The thing is, I just wanted to stop by because, well, I wanted to be sure that what we'd talked about the other day would stay between us.' Alexandria tries to laugh. 'Not that I think you're a gossip, not at all. My psychologist was always saying I needed to learn to trust people and I know that, a hundred per cent, but when I'm lying there and can't sleep, I get to imagining that the whole grade is going to find out that I scored under the norm a year ago and that Naómí's father is an abuser.'

Alexandria hesitates and waits for Vetur to say something but then it's like she doesn't trust the silence and just keeps babbling about marked society and fail bias and, in that moment, Vetur sees something in the woman she loathes. In the very next breath, she figures out what it is: a shortage of personal accountability and an excess of self-pity. This woman has no talent for seeing things from someone else's doorstep, as the old saying goes, because she's never crossed her own threshold.

'. . . and you know, you just give up, for all intensive purposes—'

'For all intents and purposes.'

Alexandria says nothing.

'For all intensive purposes what?' Alexandria asks.

'The phrase is "for all *intents* and purposes". It's a common mistake, but there's no such thing as *intensive* purposes. That's just wrong.' She says the last part louder than she means to. 'Alexandria, it pains me to have to remind you of this, but in this neighbourhood, we have to uphold certain values. We emphasise transparency here, and trust. We're a society, a *samfélag*. *Sam-*, as in co-, as in together. *Félag*, as in association, fellowship, club, union. We are not many individuals all with our own private interests, we're a collective whole. You can't just barge in here in your muddy boots and start criticising everything and everyone and play the victim and expect special treatment and demand other people bend over backwards for you because you can't be bothered to put in the slightest effort.'

'Yes, I know,' says Alexandria, looking at the floor. 'You're absolutely right. I get it, a hundred per cent.'

Vetur can't help but think of vermin.

She continues: 'I don't think it's normal for someone who failed mere months ago, and who may still be unstable, to get to waltz in here and tell the rest of us what makes for healthy and unhealthy interactions. People need to know about this kind of thing. People need to be able to respond accordingly.'

Alexandria looks at her, her eyes now wide and terrified.

'He doesn't define you!' says Vetur. 'You're safe! You got a second chance! And yet here you sit, empty-handed, waiting for you and your daughter to be kicked out!'

Vetur hears the squeak of shoe soles in the hall. The door is open.

'I suggest you take responsibility for your own life,' says Vetur. 'And for God's sake, get some therapy.'

She leaves Alexandria sitting there in the classroom, fetches her overcoat from the teacher's lounge, and strides out of the school grounds. She scans the pedestrian traffic further along the pavement, doesn't see a nice blazer, no dark hair, and then she remembers something her psychologist said a long time ago, about carrying on, about being untouchable, because Daniel feeds off her emotional turmoil, her attention, and so she slows down, stretches, tries to put on a happy face, to look like she's on top of the world, bright-eyed and bushy-tailed, it's a choice to be a victim, and she smiles to herself, as if she's remembered something funny, and hurries past 104.5 without looking in to see if Daníel is in there or not.

Then, a short distance ahead of her, she sees a tall man with a leather messenger bag and a light jacket slung over one shoulder. She makes a cone with her hands and calls to him. Húnbogi looks around and she runs up to him.

'Hi, there,' she says, short of breath. 'Want to get a drink with me?'

'Já, já,' he says, and they go back into 104.5 and there's no Daníel. She sits on the sofa next to Húnbogi, closer than she normally would. He notices and gets a bit flushed, as though her proximity is kerosene. She feels him allowing himself more liberties than he has up until now. He lets himself look at her lips when she speaks, smile when she talks, tease her.

They get another drink, then a third. They banter about what's better, drying off with a soft towel or a stiff one; he grew up with a dryer in the house and she grew up with a clothes line in the basement. She asks why he's single, and he laughs and says that's an inappropriate question, but then answers that he's just out of a six-year relationship and that the break-up was a mutual decision.

'And you?' he says, turning to her. 'Why are you footloose and fancy-free?'

'Because I'm ankle-deep in admirers!' she answers, and he shakes his head and laughs with a question in his eyes.

'Because no one yet has brought me to heel.'

Húnbogi leans back on the sofa with a suffering look on his face and she laughs way too loud; they decide to stay a little longer, order food, and one of them says maybe it's not a great idea to have another drink given that they have to teach tomorrow, they order soda water; she drinks in all the details when he speaks, his jaw, the tendons in his neck, his slender, muscular shoulders, and when he mentions some album from a thousand years ago, she says she owns a physical copy (which is a lie) and why don't they go to hers and listen to it?

Then they walk, a little drunk, to her apartment, she pretends to flip through her grandma's records – 'Weird, maybe I lent it to someone' – puts something else on the turntable and sits next to Húnbogi on the three-seater sofa, close like at 104.5, and they both fall quiet when she moves even closer, and of course, her heart starts beating a bit faster and then she's crossed the threshold, she kisses him once, pauses, her face close to his, until he kisses her back. Then they take turns kissing one another until you couldn't say who was kissing whom, and she starts to breathe faster, and he starts to breathe faster, and he has his hands under her shirt, he's holding on to her waist, leaning over her on the sofa, trailing one hand over her hips, down the outside of her thigh, and it's been so long since anyone has been this close to her, far too long, not since—

Daníel is standing over her, looking at her, watching. She's lying in bed, under the covers. She knows that under the covers she has a body that can move, she *is* a body that can move, but her body's frozen, she's not safe, he's going to attack her. It feels like her ribcage is being crushed. She tries to fill her lungs with oxygen so she can fight back.

Far, far away, on the sofa in her apartment, someone asks if something's wrong.

'Vetur,' says the voice. 'Are you okay?'

Húnbogi raises himself, one elbow on the back of the sofa, looks at her. She scrambles out from under him, runs to the door, turns the knob, it's unlocked, how could she have left it unlocked, she locks it, goes over to the window and peeks through the blinds into the car park. She leans on the kitchen counter for a few seconds, then turns on the tap, lets the water run cold, splashes her face.

'Vetur,' says Húnbogi, coming towards her in the kitchen, and when she hears her name, her mouth twists, tears spring from her eyes and she can't do a thing about it, and then something breaks, she sobs over the sink, aware that Húnbogi is standing next to her, bewildered. He rubs her back lightly but says nothing. After a moment, she manages to croak, 'I'm sorry, Húnbogi. May I ask you to leave?' and he says, 'Yes, of course.'

After he's put on his shoes, he looks at her with concern.

'Was it something I did?'

'No, not at all,' she says, drying her eyes.

'Okay. I'd still really like to see you again,' he says, hesitating with his hand on the doorknob. 'I can't stop thinking about you.'

She tries to smile, nods before she closes the door behind him and locks it as quietly as she possibly can. Then the tears take over.

—

If she had just reversed course, if she had just used a tactful voice and kept acting as an intermediary for her co-workers, been diplomatic on behalf of her co-workers, and then gradually made herself uglier, more difficult, more boring, then maybe Daníel wouldn't have felt rejected and become obsessed with her. She'd done it before, she'd stopped seeing people without actually having to break up with them, but on that particular occasion, she couldn't be bothered, she looked coldly into Daníel's face and said that maybe it would be best if he just went home. She wasn't in the mood for this right now. He stood up, his back unusually stiff, and left.

The messages started that same night, it was like a knife had been stuck between his ribs, or a key turned, and everything came tumbling out, he wrote that he'd worked at that school for years, that the whole time, the other teachers had treated him like some loser, like shit, like he was weird, they made fun of him when he was standing right there, as if he could be in on the joke, as if he could just make fun of himself, take part in his own bullying, and then in traipses Vetur in her muddy boots, thinking that after working there for a couple of months that she knows better, that he's imagining things, that he's misunderstanding, that he can't tell the difference between healthy and unhealthy interactions.

He asked if she realised how terrible she made him feel when she said these things, how he'd started questioning reality, how much bullshit he'd endured over the years and he couldn't bear it from her, that he was in love with her, that he'd been in love with her since before she ever spoke to him, before she even noticed him.

Vetur had stepped on a landmine. She wrote back that she'd talk to him the next day, once he'd calmed down, but when she got to work, he'd called in sick. She got a ride with her colleague to the office where the school had booked time slots for the teaching staff to take the empathy test. Daníel was nowhere to be seen, but that wasn't particularly notable; they only tested people one at a time and there were only ever four or five teachers in the waiting room.

That night, more messages. Couldn't she see how cruel she was, how abusive it was to make him feel like this, to make him writhe around feeling uncertain about himself and the truth of their relationship, was she actually that cold-blooded, that egocentric, that she couldn't see his side of things? Did she not care about him at all? Should he just jump off the nearest bridge?

She asked him to stop. Not to write any more. She asked him to give her time to think and then they could talk, face to face, like adults, when they'd both calmed down, when neither of them was boiling over with anger. She hoped that her reply would make him see that his accusations were angering her, too, that he should take a step back.

And then there was silence until a day and a half later, in the early hours of the morning. So this was her true nature, he wrote. This was how it was going to be. She was just like every other female, she let men crawl after her, need her, worship her, all to get over her own inferiority complex, but at whose expense? His expense. It was entirely at his expense. There he was, sitting there, a shell of himself, and she just kept living her life like nothing had happened.

He hated her, he wrote. He wished she didn't exist, that she'd never been born.

'This man is dangerous,' said her mother. 'Call the police.'

'I just need to talk to him. Try to calm him down.'

'Nothing you do will make a difference,' said her mum. 'You were nothing but good to him. Now we're going to call the police.'

The police recommended that she set up Chaperone, which she did with some reluctance. She wasn't afraid of him, not like that. He wasn't going to do anything; she knew him. She was supposed to keep a file of everything he sent her and always have Chaperone on. That way, the police would be able to access her location and recordings. If she needed evidence for a restraining order later, they'd have the camera and microphones on her wrists. If he threatened her physically, she was supposed to say nine nine nine and the police would come to her aid.

Vetur called his father, who said very little, but thanked her for calling and apologised for his son's behaviour. His dad didn't know this had happened, he'd go see him and try to reason with him.

The next few days passed in silence. Daníel didn't come to work, and the teaching staff received a memo saying that those who had not already gone for testing needed to do so within the next two weeks if they wanted to be able to renew their contracts for the coming school year. Vetur tried to still her anxiety by preparing a speech for Daníel. She spoke to the mirror and paced the floor at home. She'd say she understood him, she'd tell him she cared about him, that she hadn't meant to make him feel this way.

She fell asleep with the speech in her head.

And then she woke up. Checked her watch, it wasn't yet five-thirty. She turned on her side. Then she realised the traffic was too loud, she could hear it too well, a cold gust swept through the bedroom, and she raised her head from the pillow and saw him there, at the foot of the bed, looking at her.

His chest was rising and falling. He looked sick. The thought: *He's going to kill you.* And before she could do anything else, her body drew up into a little ball. The tiny ball only had two eyes and a heartbeat and could do nothing but lie there, defenceless, and wait for what was to come.

Laíla,

There's a fine line between being an adviser and an adversary. Our relationship dynamic has always been such that you ask for advice and I give it. In so doing, you've given me something akin to a voting interest in your life. You give me the authority to interfere by calling me every time you're faced with a decision. The issue you raise about asking questions pains me deeply – the fact that you think I'm uninterested in your life. I truly am interested and will try to take that on board. But I must say that what you wrote in your last letter wasn't fair. You say you've asked me many times over the years to stop speaking down to you, and that's simply not true. I've never heard you say one word about it before now. If I've made you feel small, then, of course, I apologise. That was not my intention. But you can't act like I'm some kind of repeat offender when I've never even been fined.

Societal values soften and harden in turn. Like fat. Like oil or butter. They heat and melt and take on new forms and congeal. All of a sudden, profile pictures on social media signal egotism, which signals a lack of empathy. All of a sudden, arguments signal aggressiveness and stupidity, which also signal a lack of empathy. Change happens so fast now it gives you a crick in the neck. So fast that those who are slow on the uptake don't even notice something's different until they're scolded for being unenlightened. And then what happens? The unenlightened go on the defensive and the enlightened wage further attacks. It's the way of the world and always has been.

Of course I'm in favour of this new mode of argumentation, which seems to me like a step forward. Of course I, like you, want to try and forestall this cycle of attack and defence, so that people can talk to one another. Of course I want us to stop this eternal debate in which the honour, reputation and image of the individual is constantly at stake, in which it's either victory or defeat, and both parties end up storming off in a fit of pique.

Last week, Róheiður came home from school and said, Mama, I changed my mind today! like she'd found money on the pavement. Maybe her generation has yet to really struggle with this, maybe the conditioning has actually taken root – that it isn't a loss to be wrong, but rather a gain. Maybe it will happen that future generations listen to each other, that their emphasis will be on the progress of the whole, rather than the glory of the individual. Personally, I have my doubts. This tendency, to want to never be wrong, is simply too bound up with power and strength. If we look to other primates – monkeys or gorillas, for example – we see that alpha morality reigns supreme for them as well. The alpha chimp gains power through the same means that a person does: a blend of physical superiority, intelligence and alliances. The other chimps bow and scrape. This is our intrinsic nature. We rally behind a leader and their views because we believe that doing so best serves our own interests. If those views are challenged, that's where a power struggle begins.

But humanity, like so often before, is trying to rise above its animal nature and perform what's called 'civilisation'. Everywhere I go, I hear the same hollow clichés. That everything's a spectrum. That nothing's black-and-white. And I agree. But the moment I venture into the grey area, the no-man's-land, that's when the discussion becomes monochrome, for or against. The moment I don't unreservedly agree with political correctness, I'm a 'wolf in sheep's clothing'.

Isn't that what you did? The moment I revealed the slightest trepidation, the moment I didn't join in with the chorus of echoes, suddenly, you couldn't substantiate your case and instead reached for the weapon closest at hand, which was to criticise the debate itself and me personally. You called time out and tried to give me a red card. But the ball's still there, alone and forgotten on the pitch, Laíla. How about you kick it? Don't you think the space between the two extremities is a bit cramped? It is in these moments, in other words, that I endanger myself in the grey area, that I really feel the total lack of dialogue that reigns in our society. It's in these moments that I experience the two poles. North Pole and South. A rift that's become so great that each of the poles speaks their own language. The poles look at the same words and then imbue them with their own meanings. Everyone points the finger at someone else, everyone's a victim, everyone's a perpetrator. People flatly refuse to listen to the other side. More and more often I see posts from otherwise intelligent people in which they declare that they're blocking anyone who has opinions that differ from their own. Or else they say: 'If X is something you support, do me a favour and unfriend me.' I think this is genuinely dangerous behaviour. To situate yourself in such a way that you only hear your own opinion and never listen to anyone who thinks the opposite. It's unhealthy. To feign critique but then behave like this. It's not possible to take a real position on anything without hearing the opposing arguments.

It's sometimes forgotten in conversation just how lazy we are at our cores. The vast majority of us approximate our opinions. We can't be bothered to do our own information gathering, to form our own opinions. It's convenient to fall in line behind a leader who persuades us. To echo their battle cries.

It saves us time. It saves us from both the work and the stalemate that comes with understanding all the angles. Haven't you noticed how uncomfortable you get when someone disagrees with you? How relieved you are when someone has the same opinion you do?

But here's the thing: even though I may be in favour of the empathy test, that doesn't mean I can't critique it. People are deceitful, above all things – you can send them to therapy ad infinitum and teach them to be well behaved and good and to untangle all their knots. You can fashion a transparent, civilised society out of plexiglass where everyone has all the 'tools' to live a 'healthy' life. But under that foundation, water is seeking cracks to seep through, under that soft fur is an animal that's greedy and cruel and thinks only of one thing: surviving. Have you never encountered that cruelty in yourself? Have you never listened to a person who's hard-up, who is perhaps stricken with depression, who needs you in order to carry on, and gotten angry, even aggressive? It is innate in us to not want to be in the same herd as those who threaten our survival, those who slow us down.

Society has, for a very long time, attempted to understand the ugliness in human beings. Consider the isolative underpinning to the Icelandic verb *að skilja*. Skilja has, of course, several distinct meanings,

the two most common being a) to understand, and
b) to separate, to divide. We try to skilja, to separate,
one thing from another – the ugly from the beautiful,
man from animal – in order to isolate it and get rid of
what we don't want. The Latin word *comprehendere*,
on the other hand, from which English, among other
languages, derives the word 'comprehend', does the
exact opposite: it means to assemble, to combine.
The prefix 'com-' is similar to the Icelandic 'sam-' and
means together, while 'prehendere' means to grasp, to
get a hold of something.

You say that the context of words, the way they
were said, has an effect on their meaning. I agree
with you completely and I apologise if I spoke down
to you. It wasn't deliberately done. But at the same
time, perhaps we need a broader lens and a wider
context in order to see what's happening here. Why
do you feel like I'm speaking down to you, whereas
I feel like I'm speaking to an equal? I have a theory
– and I hope you'll forgive me – that this is because
I have a stronger self-image than you do. Therefore,
the cumulative effect is that even though you say
things that are equally upsetting to me – that I'm a
'wolf in sheep's clothing', for example – my words
still take on more weight somehow. And I can't help
but feel that's unfair.

Tea

19.

Someone rings the bell. Eyja checks the intercom and sees a boy she doesn't know standing at the entrance.

Probably selling something.

She walks back into the living room without answering, flops on the sofa, and projects the screen back up in front of her.

Shortly after, she hears a hollow knock. Like something's bumped into the window in the vestibule.

Then the sound of breaking glass.

She looks around at the empty smoothie glasses and wine bottles and meal trays that have yet to be picked up; she grabs a dirty butter knife.

'One one two,' she whispers, holding Zoé close to her mouth.

A computerised voice answers the emergency line and asks how it can be of assistance.

'Someone is breaking into my apartment.'

The computerised voice asks if she has Chaperone, so they can access her location and camera.

She says no, whispers her address, huddles behind the sofa, and a moment later, a well-dressed boy comes out of the hall.

He's got on one of those whatever they are called.

A holomask.

He steps cautiously into the atrium.

'STOP,' she says, and comes out from behind the sofa holding up the knife.

The burglar jumps, hand on his chest, stumbles backwards, yanks a painting from the wall behind him, and runs out.

She listens to his footsteps fade down the stairwell.

Her voice shakes when she asks Zoé to call Breki.

The number is still out of service, which means she's still persona non grata.

She opens the burner account she's been using to follow them.

She lifts her wrist to her face and turns on the camera. As soon as she sees herself in the picture, she breaks down.

'Breki, can you call me? It's an emergency,' she says through her tears.

She calls her friends as she tiptoes into the vestibule and sees that the window by the front door is broken.

Her friends answer one after the other.

'There's glass everywhere,' she sobs.

They talk over one another, asking what's happened.

She walks away from the open front door and into the bedroom, where she locks herself in.

She somehow manages to tell them what happened, and they wait on the line with her until two police officers get there, a man and a woman.

She repeats the chain of events. She describes the boy, and they record her witness statement.

Then they ask what security system she has, if she's considered getting Chaperone or marking her home.

'No,' she answers without looking at them.

Her throat hurts from crying and her eyes are swollen.

The woman sits down next to her, asks if there's a particular reason for that.

'I don't care for surveillance,' she answers.

'I don't care for having a face-lock camera recording whoever comes and goes.'

'I believe in personal freedom.'

The policewoman says that's an understandable position. But it means that she's also vulnerable. There are a lot of break-ins on unmarked floors.

'Yes, right, so you're saying that it's my fault,' says Eyja, finally looking up.

'It's my fault I don't have a security system.'

'It's my fault someone invaded my home and threatened my life and it's my fault I was fired and my husband cheated on me and my parents neglected me.'

'You all blame me, the lot of you.'

'You will sooner or later, anyway.'

Not at all, says the policewoman. The burglar is the only one who is at fault here. All she meant was that it would be possible, next time, to prevent a burglar from making it so far.

'This fucking society is going to hell!' Eyja tries to say.

'Nowhere is safe!' she tries to say.

'Why don't you *do* something!' she stammers.

The policewoman puts an arm around her shoulder and says over and over that it's okay. She says this is normal, first comes the shock and then come the tears. It's nothing to be ashamed of.

The policewoman keeps talking, blathering something about trauma and a sense of security. Her voice becomes overwhelming, a piercing sound that closes in on Eyja.

She can't think.

'I want to be alone now,' she blurts out and the policewoman stops mid-sentence. 'Thank you for your help.'

The policewoman asks if she's sure, whether there's anyone on the way. A spouse, a family member? Children?

'Yes, they're all on the way.'

The policewoman stands up. The policeman encourages her to engage a security system and seek crisis counselling.

Finally, he calls. As soon as she hears his voice, she starts sobbing again.

'Breki,' she says. 'I don't know what to do.'

He gets there half an hour later. He's wearing a jacket, blue jeans and sunglasses.

She's sitting on the sofa with a blanket wrapped around her.

He asks what in the world happened as he hops through the open front door and over the shards of glass.

She hurries to him and starts crying.

He puts his arms around her, and she sobs into the chest she knows so well.

For a moment, the present collapses into the past.

Like the corners of a folded duvet. Everything that has happened in between disappears into the creases.

She feels him breathing her in.

Your perfume, he says. He says he smells her scent everywhere.

She looks up and he looks into her eyes and then slowly releases her from the embrace.

With reluctance, she thinks.

He asks if she wants anything to drink. Water? Tea? Coffee?

She shakes her head. Wraps the blanket more tightly around her. Dries her face with her free hand.

He looks around the living room at the meal trays and bottles. Asks if Inga Lára and Natalía and Eldey are on their way. Asks again what happened.

'I . . .' she says. 'Þórir fired me and then there was a burglar.'

Breki raises his eyebrows. He runs a hand through his hair, stops at his crown and massages his scalp.

He asked why Þórir fired her. They'd always worked so well together.

'I wouldn't sleep with him,' she says with a deep sniffle.

What? says Breki. He asks if she's telling the truth.

'Of course I'm telling the truth. Þórir came to my door on a work trip to Toronto and then he fired me two weeks later. Why wouldn't I be telling the truth?'

Because, says Breki, she tends to lie about people who give up on her.

Because he's been hearing lies about himself every time he turns around.

The most unbelievable people seem to think he'd cheated on her with Katrín.

He's angry now. He stands over her with one hand on his hip like he always does when he's mad.

'Breki . . .' she says.

She cheated on *him*! he shouts.

He met Katrín *months* after he moved out!

He says Katrín almost lost her job after all the goddamn lies and bullshit she's been spreading around.

He takes his face in both hands. He says he can't believe he let himself be tricked yet again. What would his psychologist say?

'I was mad at you!' she says. 'I'm sorry!'

Yeah, says Breki, just like she'd been mad at all her exes.

Just like she was mad at her father. And then lied about him beating her when she was younger.

'He could just as well have!' she says, getting up from the sofa.

'And you could have just as well have cheated on me! The pain would be exactly the same!'

Breki looks at her, opens his mouth like he's going to say something, then shakes his head and storms out.

She's bleeding. She lifts her finger to her face. Squints.

Goddamn her vision. She can't see a thing.

She feels tentatively and pulls out a shard of glass.

She scoops more shards onto one of the dirty meal trays.

When most of the glass is on the tray, she shakes it and sees blood visible on the shards.

Wonderful!

She puts a lid on the tray, which is caked with congealed, orange sauce.

The taxi comes shortly after she calls.

The driver tries to strike up a conversation with her. At first, she attempts to signal that she's not in the mood to chat by giving single-syllable responses. But he's curious.

Asks question after question after question.

'I'm not in the mood to chat,' she says with a hiccup.

And then suddenly, they're outside the office tower.

Which will soon be her *former* workplace.

'Wait for me,' she says holding the tray as she slams the door.

Her key still works, no problem.

She can't get rid of these goddamn hiccups. She holds her breath in the elevator. Gasps for breath on the seventh floor.

She gets out on the ninth.

His office is unlocked.

As if he has nothing to hide!

She plucks a few shards of glass off the meal tray and takes them into the bathroom, rinses them in the sink with soap.

Then she kneels under his desk and holds out her hand.

'When the bough breaks,' she says as she scatters a few of the shards across the floor.

She bumps her head on the desk as she stands up.

'Ow!'

Then her eyes drift to the overcoat hanging on the coat tree to her right.

She walks over to the coat and sprinkles a few shards of glass into the crease of the rolled-up sleeve.

Pats them down carefully so they won't fall out.

When she gets home, she looks at the clock.

Not late at all! Only eight!

She opens another bottle and calls the police.

'Yes, good evening,' she says when they pick up. 'Two officers came to my apartment today. Because of a break-in. Someone broke into my apartment. I think I know who it was.'

And then, everything is dry.

Her head is dry.

Her body is dry.

Her skin. Her mouth.

She tries to move and can feel that she's naked.

She opens her eyes and sees that she's alone.

Zoé's battery is dead.

She closes her eyes again and has a hazy memory of a body on top of her yesterday, Gylfi's hook-tongue. She lies in bed and tries to remember the day before.

Did she go to the office?

Why?

Then the bell rings.

It's a man with a pot belly. Short, grey hair.

He says he's here with new glass for the window in the vestibule.

Did she order new glass? She doesn't remember doing so. Although she probably did. He points to the tray with three smoothie glasses outside her front door and asks if it's supposed to be there.

She picks up the tray without answering.

Then it's like he can't stop staring at her.

He points to the window with his index finger and asks if the break-in was because of the thing in the news? Did those bastards break her window?

'What news?'

He says maybe he's mixed her up with someone else.

He gets embarrassed and mumbles something into his chest.

She turns around and locks the door between the hall and the vestibule.

She hurries into the bedroom and plugs in Zoé.

Her watch turns on immediately. She projects her portal and sinks into bed as the messages and videos pile up in front of her.

Þórir sent her a gram.

Her friends sent her grams.

Fjölnir and Kári did too.

Her mum is asking her to call.

She opens the first news site she thinks of and sees her own face appear with a picture of the firm in the background.

20.

Tristan runs as fast as his fucking feet will take him down the stairs, down into the basement, where he changes his jacket and then runs out to the delivery truck and drives straight to the underground garage. He changes cars there and drives to another underground garage and then he goes up to the shopping centre that's above the garage and swaps out his clothes in the bathroom, out of his collared shirt and into a big sweater and comfortable pants. His undershirt is so wet that he throws it in the bin, then he looks at the shirt in the bin and changes his mind, pulls it back out and stuffs it in his backpack.

He splashes water on his face and dries it on his sweater. The light in the bathroom is way too bright. Blinding white. His stomach is fucking killing him. His mouth tastes like metal and he spits and sees blood in the white sink. He freaks out when he sees it and his heartbeat goes up to one hundred and seventy and Zoé chirps and he sits down on the lid of the toilet.

'Somehow, it all turns out somehow,' he says and imagines that he's in the elevator in their old apartment building and can't do anything, he can't go faster than the elevator, the elevator is carrying him, he is safe in the elevator, for a few seconds, no one comes in, no one goes out. 'I'm in an elevator,' he says and breathes in. 'I'm in an elevator,' he says and breathes out.

He runs down the steps when he comes out of the building and waits for the H next to a busy street. The H finally comes, and he stands near the exit, holding the little plastic noose hanging from the ceiling. He senses the cameras in the train, they know where he is and where he's going. A cop car will be waiting for him when he gets out and then it's fucking finito.

'Excuse me,' says someone.

He looks around and sees an old man who could be his grandpa. The man leans in close, like he's going to tell him a secret.

'I just wanted to tell you I'm really impressed with the gumption of you boys. Telling your stories. It's so important. That people understand your situation, that your hands are tied. That video was both needed and necessary. *Ég hvet þig til dáða.*'

'Thank you,' Tristan tries to say but doesn't get it all out, the last syllable is silent. The old man gives him a thumbs-up and then the H stops, and the old man slowly steps out.

'Zoé,' says Tristan. 'What does hvetja til dáða mean?'

Að hvetja einhvern til dáða, says Zoé in his ears. *To motivate someone, to cheer someone on, to encourage. Example: Ég hvet þig til dáða. Meaning: You keep up the good work.* When he gets to the harbour, he finds Eldór in D1. He tells him there's nothing in the truck now and that he's out.

'What, why?' says Eldór without looking away from the container he's steering with a remote.

Tristan tells him what happened and Eldór laughs his loud hyena laugh when Tristan describes the old lady with the knife and how her fifty-year-old tit just like, fucking popped out of her robe.

'But you had a mask and gloves and all that, right?'

'Yeah, what do you think I am?'

'Dude, it's not a problem.'

'I just can't, man. I feel like the cops can see every fucking step I take. There are cameras everywhere. I don't have the fucking nerves for this. I've started spitting blood.'

'What? Blood?'

'Yeah.'

'Do you think you've got some disease or—?'

'Yeah, I got a bacterial infection in my stomach a long time ago and the pain gets worse when you take trex, þú veist, and I'm stressed out and whatever. I can't deal, man.'

'Fuck.'

'Yeah.'

'What are you going to do?'

'I don't know. But I'm done cleaning.'

After work, Viktor tells him to get in the car and Tristan knows Victor is going to give him some money.

'How's it going finding a new job?'

He doesn't look at Tristan when he says it. He looks out at the car park in front of them, calm, relaxed.

'Viktor. I'm sorry, really. I know I'm super fucking ungrateful. I'm just so stressed out all the time, especially after the container in November. I have to find something more low-key.'

Viktor smiles and Tristan doesn't trust that smile at all. It's the same smile he gave Wojciech when Wojciech asked for a time out.

'You didn't answer the question. How's it going, finding a new job?'

'Not good.'

Viktor nods and then hands Tristan a little book with his money folded inside it. Tristan takes it and sticks it in his pocket.

'You owe me,' says Viktor.

He limps home. His stomach can't take any fucking more. The stabbing pain is fucking unbearable. It's like he swallowed a razor blade or something. He tries to breathe, but it's like his lungs are much smaller, like they're taking in much less oxygen for all intensive purposes. He counts the money from Viktor. He might just make it, but only if Ólafur Tandri doesn't press charges. He thinks about that fucking old bag today and how fucking lucky he is that he wasn't taken into custody and that he doesn't have a record, given how many houses he's cleaned. He promises himself to never, ever clean again. But he's promised himself that a bunch of times before.

He wakes up in his bedroom. It's almost morning. His

stomach aches and it hurts to swallow but the stabbing feeling is gone. He eats a bowl of cereal as slowly as he can and takes a trex with it. It doesn't take long to kick in.

It's a week and one day until the vote. Eight days. Eight fucking days.

He goes to work and tries to think as little as he can and the next day (seven days), he goes out to see the apartments. The first one is somewhere out in Fossvogur and it's alright and the second one is in Hafnarfjörður and is less nice but also fine. He makes an offer on both of them and takes some pills that Eldór gives him on Sunday (six days) to zone out, to make the time pass, and when he wakes up on Monday (five), his pillow is wet with spit. He calls both estate agents around lunchtime and neither of them have showed the offers to the owners yet, but they promise he'll have an answer the next day.

On Tuesday (four), one calls, and on Wednesday (three), the other does. Both say the same thing, that his offer was rejected and here's the counter-offer. Both are way too fucking high. When he gets the second answer, he kicks a container as hard as he can, and Wojciech looks up when the metal rumbles.

Something gives inside him, like a wet cardboard box that rips on the bottom and everything tumbles out. He starts shaking. He imagines himself homeless, imagines himself as a hobo, as a junkie on the street. He's seen guys go that way, guys around him, people he's known who have ended up on the street, barefoot and bloody.

Ólafur Tandri calls while he's at work. Tristan stands completely still and stares at the name. He waits until it stops ringing.

After work, he goes to see the last apartment. It's on Hverfisgata, right by where Eldór lives, also in an old hotel, just one room with a little kitchen in a corner. When the estate agent opens the door, it's disgusting, it smells disgusting and everything that should be white is brown. It's on the ground floor, right next to the road, so you can hear all the cars outside like they're driving through the walls. There's a hole in the floor of the shower and he can hear a scratching sound beneath him.

They stop and Tristan looks at the estate agent and the agent gives the shower floor a little kick. The scratching stops and it's totally silent, but then a giant fucking tail pokes out of the hole and both Tristan and the agent try to stay cool, but they get the fuck out of the bathroom as fast as they fucking can.

'You could definitely offer well under the asking price,' says the agent. 'It's been on the market for so long.'

'Oh yeah?' says Tristan, looking around. 'Okay. Good to know.'

He sits on his mattress at home. Then he tells Zoé to make the call.

'Hi, I'm busy. I'll talk to you later,' says Rúrik.

'Are you pissed at me?'

'What do you think?'

'I had to do it.'

'You didn't have to fucking do it like that.'

'Sorry. I just got so stressed. I had no idea they would ask about you,' he says. 'But I found an apartment for us.'

'Us? I don't have any fucking money, Tristan.'

'You think I don't know that? But you still have to live somewhere when you get out. It's just one room, but there'll be enough room for both of us there. We can just put a little bed on each side and then—'

'Nei,' says Rúrik. 'No. Go home to Mum and finish school.'

'I can't live there, you know that.'

'Yes, you can live there. Take the test, get help to get off the trex, and finish school.'

'I'm sorry I talked about you in the video. I just panicked.'

'Tristan, don't butt in or try to crash my plans like you always do.'

'But we have to buy an apartment if we're going to fucking survive!'

'What do you think is actually happening? We'll always be able to find a place to live.'

'Nei, seriously, Rúrik. You've got to believe me. There are so many guys that are homeless now, you wouldn't fucking believe it.'

'Goddamn it, Tristan, don't start telling me the way things are. I know a lot more about it than you do. If you need to find another room before the end of the month, I know at least two hotels that rent to unmarked guys.'

'Yeah, okay, but then what? Then after a year, those hotels

will decide to mark and by then we won't be able to buy an apartment any more.'

'Of course we'll be able to buy an apartment. You are so fucking stupid sometimes.'

'Maybe the banks will decide to change the rules so that if people don't pass, then they can't get a loan.'

'Stop being so fucking childish. The banks *want* your money. Why are they going to ban thousands of people from giving them money?'

'You just never know, you know? We need to be safe. Especially you.'

'Especially me?'

'Yeah, þú veist, because of the test and all that.'

'Stop being so fucking worried about me. I am working on my shit. And you need to work on yours, too. Take the test. Go home to Mum. Stop working at the harbour.'

'But—'

'I've got to go,' says Rúrik. 'I'll talk to you later.' Then he hangs up.

Tristan takes two trex at once and smokes the jurt from Eldór on top of that and lies down and feels his body relaxing, little by little, like it's lifting up for all intensive purposes. For a second his heart stops being a giant fucking shipping container and his body goes back to being a giant swimming pool he's floating in, his soul is made of vapour and he thinks about that disgusting apartment on Hverfisgata with the rat and the smell, he has to make an offer on it, yeah, he'll offer on it tomorrow and call Ólafur Tandri and tell him he'll go to fucking therapy if he doesn't have to pay the fine. It's the only way he's going to make it. He'll fix up the apartment with Rúrik, yeah, paint it and change out the bottom of the shower and maybe the floor or something to get rid of the smell, there must be videos on the internet that teach you how to replace a floor, and then he can focus on getting a new job, and when he has a new job, then maybe he won't always be so stressed and he can focus on getting off the trex, yeah, it's okay to get help for it, he doesn't have to take the test to go to that kind of rehab, and finally, when he manages to quit the trex, then he can maybe finish school, he can study something that will let him work from home so he never has to get that EE EE EE sound in his face ever again. Maybe when he's back in school, he can call Sunneva and explain everything, and maybe she'll see him and believe him, and maybe she'll be his girlfriend and he'll get to kiss light every night, yeah, he's on the right track, this is happening, he's going to make it, he's definitely going to make it, but what is that music, there's some kind of music all around him, and he tries to lift his head but he can't and then the music gets louder, it's coming from his watches, and then some screen projects above him, and there's a blinking red light, and Zoé says something about his heartbeat and then he hears that the music is actually sirens, marvellous glorious divine sirens, and they're spinning like the blades in one of those meat grinders or a blender or any of those things that turn food into mash and coffee into powder, and he sinks into the sound, he goes through the meat grinder and the sirens, the blades are mashing him, pulping him.

21.

Zoé tells her to go out and get some exercise. Zoé tells her to bathe. Zoé tells her to eat, to drink water, that her progesterone and oestrogen levels are low, she needs to be mindful of her decisions and social interactions. Húnbogi sends her a message, asks if she's feeling better. Once she's able to start thinking clearly again, fragments of the past week come back to her, one by one: Naómí's teeth, Alexandria's shoulders, Húnbogi's face in close-up the moment before she kissed him, snatches of things she said. She calls the headmistress and resigns from her position as the Quarter School's social studies teacher.

'Are you sure, Vetur?' asks the headmistress. 'All of us are really happy with you here, the teaching staff and the parents and kids. If this is a question of sick leave, we can work something out.'

'Thank you, but yes, I'm sure. Sorry I've taken so many sick days. I'll be back after the weekend and will finish out the semester.'

She needs to talk to Alexandria, apologise to her. But she puts it off, has a phone appointment with her psychologist, tells her what's happened, tries as best she can to hold herself accountable. Together, they analyse her behaviour, which actions were driven by what, what was transference, emotional detachment. After half an hour or so, they both fall silent.

'Vetur,' says her psychologist gently. 'Might it be that you're waiting for a confrontation with Daníel?'

'Maybe. Deep down.'

'Yes,' agrees her psychologist. 'I think you need to begin a kind of grieving process with respect to that narrative. What's most important is that you get your life back on track.'

'How do I do that?'

'It's possible that the best thing for you would be a change of scenery. Maybe you could apply for a doctoral programme abroad somewhere?'

'But isn't that just avoiding the problem?'

'Not necessarily. You're working through your trauma. You have strong family ties. Daníel is clearly seeking professional help on his side.'

'That doesn't mean he's not still dangerous.'

'Definitely not. But he did pass the empathy test, that's something.'

'But when I come home after the doctoral programme, am I just supposed to trust he won't do it again? It's like building a house next to a volcano.'

'Yes,' says her psychologist, looking past the camera. 'But people do that. People build their homes next to volcanoes every day.'

Vetur can sink into the memory like a hot bath, feel the texture of her pillowcase when she rolls over in bed – sinking into the moment before she sees him standing over her:

His hair is dirty and sticks to his head. That's the first thing she notices. His chest rises and falls. He looks sick. The thought: He's going to kill you. And then reality is yanked out from under her. Everything becomes far too clear. Everything becomes far too slow. The big picture crumbles into minutia: loud breathing. Stiff back. She hears him say: 'Sorry I woke you,' and, 'I wanted to give you those.'

He points to the dresser by the bedroom door. There's a bouquet of roses. Cheap, from a service station. She hears him say: 'I haven't been able to sleep for four days.' Then the words start pouring out of him and that's when the memory gets hazy. The past year has blurred his speech. Each sentence bleeds into the next, becomes one continuous line, like when a sparkler is twirled in a circle: 'I'm sorry, I wasn't myself, I haven't been able to sleep, I love you so much, I can't believe I've messed this up, you're the best thing that's ever happened to me, you make me feel like I'm normal, ever since I was little, I've felt like something was wrong with me, every time I make a new friend, I expect them to stop wanting anything to do with me when they see how ridiculous I am, I can't lose you, Vetur, I love you so much, you're the best thing that's ever happened to me, I'll stop talking shit about people at work, I'll see a psychologist, I'll work on my issues, I didn't mean anything I said, I wasn't myself.'

After this speech, he takes a few steps closer. As soon as he does, it's like her body twitches back into action. She recoils across the bed, stands up on the other side. There's something weighing on her chest. Something so heavy she can't speak.

He stops and looks her dead in the eye. All kinds of emotions flit across his face: puzzlement, disappointment, disbelief.

'Vetur, I'll do anything, I'm just so messed up, I'm so scared that people are going to leave me, I didn't mean any of the stuff I wrote, I love you.'

'Hush,' she says, but it comes out as a whisper. 'Just stop,' she whispers, and she realises these are the wrong words, she should say something else, that he needs to leave and she's afraid of him, but these thoughts don't come to her in words but rather in electric waves pulsing through her body and skull. She points to the balcony door and tries to find the sounds that will form the right meaning.

'Goodbye,' she whispers and stabs her finger in the direction of the balcony. 'Goodbye!'

And then he goes crazy. He tears at his hair and his hands turn to fists and he screams and bursts into tears. He says: 'I can't go back!' He says: 'I'll never get over this!' He says: 'I can't just find some other girlfriend! I won't survive this! Don't you get it?' and for some ludicrous reason, Vetur begins to laugh, a neurotic, shaking laughter, her brain is sending the wrong signals to her face, Daníel's expression contorts and Vetur backs into a corner and the waves of laughter are still rolling through her. Then, as if Daníel has to do something with all the anger in his body, he kicks the desk chair, the chair flies into the wall, he looks at Vetur and is about to say something but starts crying again and then opens his arms wide and takes a step towards her and then she remembers that Chaperone is on because the police recommended that she set up Chaperone. 'Nine nine nine,' she says and immediately sirens start wailing from both her wrists, and the sirens are the most difficult part of the memory, the sirens that underline her helplessness, her desperation, those ear-splitting sirens. Daníel puts his hands over his ears and Vetur runs past him, yanks open the front door and beats wildly on her neighbour's door across the hall, looks back to see Daníel gazing at her from inside the apartment, then turning on his heel, climbing over the balcony railing, and hopping onto the grass below.

Her neighbour lets her in. Leads her to the sofa while she sobs uncontrollably and calls her parents. The police come and take a statement from her and get permission to use the recordings from her watches. Almost everything was caught on video – how he reached his arm through her bedroom window and opened the balcony door from the inside, how he paused in the doorway to watch her sleep, how he crept over to the dresser and arranged the roses there. And how he stiffened when he saw she'd woken up. The next day, she pressed charges against him, and a restraining order was put in place for the next four weeks; Daníel was informed he had to stay at least fifty metres away from her and that he was not to contact her in any way. Vetur was told he'd be monitored by Spotter, which allowed the police direct access to his location, and that for the next four weeks, police would receive a notification if he got too close to her. Vetur stayed with her parents and her father drove her to and from work until the school year ended a week later, and with every passing day, she got bolder; she believed it was over, believed in her heart that he'd crossed those boundaries inadvertently, so she went back to her apartment and invited friends or family to come over every night. And then she saw him in the black Benz, on the other side of the field, and that was when the gravity of the situation finally hit her.

She didn't see him again after the second restraining order, but she still couldn't shake the feeling that he was there somewhere, just outside her peripheral vision, just beyond the two hundred metres, watching her, waiting. It took her months to be able to sleep alone in her apartment again after that, and even longer to be able to walk around the neighbourhood in broad daylight. She bought heavy venetian blinds and pulled the curtains across all the windows. And grew accustomed to the dark.

The week passes. She gets phone calls from both the pro- and the anti-markers, urging her to vote on Saturday. Her friends come over, spend the evenings with her. Another protest breaks out in Austurvöllur Square in front of Alþingi, and she follows the news distractedly, as if it has nothing to do with her. On Friday, she calls Húnbogi and tells him the whole story, everything from Daníel and her PTSD to Alexandria. Húnbogi listens without asking anything and she apologises for how she acted.

'Don't feel bad. Really. Don't worry about it,' he says.

'I do feel bad, really bad. I feel like I've swallowed you whole and then vomited you right back out.'

'Classy metaphor.'

'I've got a crush on you,' says Vetur.

'I've got a crush on you, too,' says Húnbogi.

'Would you like to come over?'

'Now?'

'Yes.'

'No, but I'll come over sometime when it isn't almost midnight.'

'When?'

'Tomorrow?'

'Okay.'

She looks around after she hangs up with Húnbogi. It's sparkling clean thanks to her mum, who has been coming by and cleaning up every day, tidying the kitchen and vac-uuming. But it's dark in here, the bright evening sun only a pink stripe between the blinds and the window frame. Vetur walks to the kitchen window and peeks through the blinds. Outside, the sunset is luminous, the sky violet, the cottony cloudbanks a fiery red, and all of this is reflected in the quasi-transparent, silvery levee that encircles the city and runs an extra loop around the Viðey Quarter. She opens the blinds, and the evening light floods the kitchen for the first time in months.

Vetur steps back from the window, backs out of the kitch-en with her arms crossed.

'I'm going to trust you,' she says to the kitchen.

She turns on her heel and heads towards the bedroom. She walks gingerly, pauses in the doorway. She looks over the room, looks at the bed and the bedside table, the dresser, the clothes rack, the curtains that conceal the balcony door and bedroom windows. She closes her eyes, inhales deeply, exhales and tries to relax her body. For a whole year, she's slept unsoundly in this bed, woken abruptly again and again to look frantically towards the balcony. She's struggled, she's fought, so as not to lose, so as not to be defeated by Daniel or to fear her own self.

She scans her body for uneasiness and finds it, that rock-hard ball in her chest with a pulse entirely its own, different from her heartbeat, a different rhythm and a different nature. She breathes in and relaxes, breathes out and relaxes and envisions that the relaxation is trust and that trust is acid that eats away at the ball. She imagines the sizzling when the acid attacks the ball, the foam and the bubbles. Then she opens her eyes. She doesn't feel good in here. She associates the bedroom with being unsafe.

'I don't trust you,' she says to the bedroom.

The moment she says it, her fear starts to split at the seams.

'I'm going to sell you,' she says, and the split becomes a hole.

'I'm going to move!' she says and laughs. She looks at her watch; still standing there in the doorway, she asks Zoé to call her mum and tells her the news. Her mum says Great, her voice cracking a little, as if she's been waiting for this for a long time, and then says that tomorrow they can call an estate agent together. After Vetur hangs up, she walks around the room, on both a high and a low ebb at the same time, and she starts to imagine where she might move. An old feeling washes over her without warning – freedom, an endless, childlike freedom – like she's standing on a bridge and watching the sky and sea run together. She heads towards the bathroom to undress for bed and then she hears something, an indistinct scraping at the front door. She freezes in her tracks, looks automatically at the doorknob, which doesn't move. Nothing happens. She sighs inwardly and is about to go back into the bathroom when she hears the sound again, scraping metal. She looks back at the knob and no, she's not imagining it, this is reality, there's a creaking coming from the gold doorknob. And then it turns, slowly, silently, a half circle one way and then back again.

22.

i always knew there was something off about her

send this insect straight back 2 the rock she lives under ideally for the rest of her life – no point in ta king any chances!!

Locking her up her would be way too expensive. A bullet only costs 250kr :)

'who has in recent years become a well-known figure in green investment circles'!!! Here you have it, folks: the cracks are showing – the system is broken!!!

Jesus. I'm *this* close to losing all faith in humanity reading some of these comments. Read the article, people. All it says is that this unfortunate woman was fired shortly after her firm was marked. That proves nothing. Dismissal from a job isn't proof of failure and even if she did fail the test, that wouldn't tell us anything about whether she'd actually done anything wrong! Let's pump the brakes, hmm? Takk.

One more black sheep culled from the flock. This is the reason we all need to vote YES on the mark on Saturday.

—

Þórir sends her a gram. He's sitting in his office with his window view behind him and looking straight into the camera.

He thanks her for the broken glass and says it was nice working with her.

He says he's been in touch with EcoZea and told them that the situation has changed.

He tells her to have a nice life. Then the gram ends.

what did she do??? it doesnt say anywhere,,, the media acts like it runs this country icelandic media is so biased god i pity this poor innosent lady

She finally gets hold of EcoZea and tries to explain, but the door has closed. Unfortunately, they say, they're no longer interested.

Dear Eyja, you probably don't remember me, but we briefly worked together at B&R, back in the old days. It's horrifying to see the court of public opinion tarnishing a person's reputation like this. My thoughts are with you during this difficult time. Best, JHJ

Gylfi doesn't answer her calls or her messages.

I don't know her at all, but she seems totally normal and decent. That's just the way it is, I guess.

Inga Lára says maybe she should think about going abroad for a while.

Somewhere in the south.

Where it's warm and she doesn't know anyone.

Natalía says that's a really good idea.

She knows a woman who owns a gorgeous place on a Greek island.

She can put her in touch.

Dear Eyja, I just want to say that you're not alone in this. Feel free to stop by one of our meetings any time, you'll be welcomed with open arms. Warmly, Magnús Geirsson.

Fjölnir calls.

Invites her to start a firm with him and Alli.

They'd make a fucking great team, the three of them.

They know the market inside out.

It's such a relief when the test exposes this kind of rabble. They shouldn't be allowed to run riot across our country.

Her mum calls. In the background, she hears her dad say not to waste her breath.

Dearest Eyja, it's difficult to see you treated so unfairly. Let me know if there's anything I can do to help. Eldey.

Gylfi sends her a message.

He says his wife found out about them.

Her friend recognised Eyja from the papers.

She'd seen the two of them at a restaurant and then getting into a taxi together.

He says he has to try to repair his marriage.

He apologises.

He wishes her well.

This woman treated my friend like garbage when they were at university together. I've rarely been as relieved as I was when they broke up.

Breki doesn't call. Breki doesn't answer.

fuck this fucling witch hhunt

The car stops and Zoé says she's reached her destination.

Where is she?

Oh, here.

The handrail's made of this sort of . . . tablecloth plastic. Weird.

There's not a sound in the stairwell.

She has to put the perfume down on the carpeted floor while she finds the keys.

She stumbles into the light switch in the stairwell and freezes when the light turns on.

She waits for ever. For ev-er.

Until the light automatically switches off again.

She's got the right key. Here it is.

Why isn't it working?

She tries turning the knob again.

Looks around.

Fuck!! She's on the wrong floor again.

She picks the perfume up off the floor and is about to go up to the next floor but stumbles over the belt of her silk robe.

She tries to break her fall with her hands, but they're full of keys and perfume and so she awkwardly sticks out an elbow and tumbles headfirst to the carpeted floor.

She lies there, on the stairs. Her body is in an absurd position, but she keeps lying there.

She's bombarded by thoughts, but then she imagines she's wearing a helmet to protect her.

She's bombarded by feelings, but then she imagines she's wearing a suit of armour that completely covers her and keeps them from getting in.

She lies on the stairs.

Then. Slowly, calmly, she pushes up with her hands underneath her and scrambles to her feet.

She takes a cautious step towards his apartment.

Their apartment: Breki and the cow.

The key slips easily into the lock.

Now it's like butter.

She listens before she opens the door a crack onto the vestibule.

She closes one of her eyes so she can see better.

Stretches her arm through the crack, finds his jacket, and sprays the inside of the collar.

Then she hears something.

Someone inside the apartment says, Halló?

It's Breki.

It's Breki.

It's Breki.

She leaves the door open and leaps down the stairs.

The stairwell light clicks on.

A policeman appears in front of the building as she reaches the ground floor.

Fuck!

She's about to turn back, but then she hears Breki on the floor above. He calls down the stairwell, asks who's there.

She hears the high-pitched *zzz* of the intercom when someone buzzes the policeman in.

'Evening,' she says with her most ingratiating smile as she hurries past the policeman.

Breki asks again who's there.

She picks up the pace and the policeman says, Wait.

She opens the first door and then the next.

She's made it outside, under the wide-open sky.

She starts walking briskly, away, past the police car.

Someone says, Hold up, friend.

Someone grabs her arm.

'I'm not your friend.'

It's another cop.

A woman.

She tells her to calm down. Holds on to her.

'Let me go. Let me go!'

She tries to scratch the policewoman, but she twists Eyja's arm behind her.

She falls to her knees.

The policeman takes her other arm.

'What do you think you're doing?'

Breki's wearing a T-shirt and jeans. He's barefoot.

There's a young woman behind him. Light red hair and a pretty face.

Not the cow, someone else.

The woman's scared. 'Who's that?' she asks. Her arms are crossed over her chest.

'What, you've got a new fucking cow?' she asks, laughing at Breki.

He looks so dramatic.

He says that's his neighbour.

He turns to the neighbour woman and asks what's going on.

The policeman asks which one of them is Vetur.

The neighbour woman says she's Vetur.

'*Vetur*,' says Eyja. 'Winter? Who the fuck names their kid *Winter*?'

Vetur the neighbour woman pretends not to hear her. She says she called the police because someone had tried to open her door. And it wasn't the first time.

The policewoman looks down at Eyja, asks if they can release her, asks if she's going to behave herself.

'I'm not a three-year-old,' she answers.

The policewoman says she can't hear her.

'I am not three years old!' Then she sighs. 'Já, já, I'll behave.'

The cops help her to her feet and let go of her.

Breki asks what she's holding.

'Nothing.'

Breki asks if she took something.

'No, it's mine!'

The policewoman asks her to show them what's in her hand. The policewoman tells her to show them what's in her hand.

Vetur the neighbour woman keeps standing in the doorway, arms crossed.

'Something's got you really scared,' Eyja says to her.

Breki says her name.

She looks him in the eye.

She sighs and holds out her open palm with the perfume and his spare keys on it.

23.

On Monday, five days before the referendum, they're at forty-nine per cent in favour. They look at the numbers in a sombre silence. They meet quickly. They eat quickly. They talk quickly. They're sweating in their boots.

Óli still hasn't heard from the boy.

'He's not going to answer,' says Óli on Tuesday morning.

'Give him two more days,' says Sólveig, cutting up Dagný's food on a violet plate. 'Then it will have been a week. If he hasn't answered by Wednesday, you can just call him then.'

'He's trying to stonewall. He's buying himself time.'

'Óli, c'mon. What's the worst that'll happen? This referendum doesn't hinge on this one particular story.'

'That interview of his got over a hundred thousand views, Sólveig. People have a right to know.'

'What time are the debates tonight?'

'Don't change the subject.'

'Okay, but really, what time are they?'

'Right after the news. Around seven-thirty.'

'We know,' says Magnús Geirsson when the interviewer gives him the floor, 'that the marking mandate is going to bring about another economic recession. We know that the marking mandate is a violation of the United Nations' Universal Declaration of Human Rights. We know that the marking mandate is going to have terrible consequences for the most vulnerable among us. Incidents of domestic violence are at an all-time high in Iceland. As is unemployment. Police discrimination and profiling are on the rise. This cannot happen. This *cannot happen.*'

He pounds his fist on the table to emphasise his last words. The programme's host looks at Salóme and Salóme smiles, bobs her head slightly before responding.

'Thank you for that, Magnús,' says Salóme. 'As so often before, it seems we've based our campaigns on entirely different information. I'd argue that the economy is blossoming at present. The króna has never been stronger. The national debt is at an all-time low. Iceland is carving out a niche for itself on the international stage in ethical, green commerce. But what's also happening is that a certain historical power shift is taking place in our country. I can well understand that your supporters, who clearly have interests to protect, are apprehensive. Finally, we have a reliable tool for determining who can be trusted with our conutry's financial assets. The public no longer wants to do business with a handful of individuals who have repeatedly committed moral crimes at great cost to the nation. We don't want this any more. We want a better society. We deserve a better society.'

She pauses briefly for effect but holds up a finger to keep the floor.

'Regarding our most vulnerable groups, I have but one

thing to say: we at the Icelandic Psychological Association have, in collaboration with the National Institute of Mental Health, worked day and night to strengthen the infrastructure of the mental-health system so that no one falls between the ship and the pier, as the saying goes.

'We have rehabilitation centres. We have individualised treatment options. We have support reps and psychologists, psychiatrists and neuropsychologists, all available to the public, free of charge. This is truly a watershed moment in the history of our country, and it unfortunately comes as no surprise that abusers are sitting at home in despair. But imagine to yourself that in just a few months' time, we could know where these abusers are and offer them help. We could contact their partners and offer them assistance, whether short-term or otherwise. We could change the world for the better.'

His father calls after the debate.

'Well, she made a hash of that, didn't she, your boss? That was painful to watch.'

'Salóme?' says Óli. 'And here we were so pleased with her.'

'Do you actually think', continues his father, 'that the ruling class is going to hand over their power, just like that? No. They're going to find whatever loopholes they can and then it'll be business as usual, like nothing's changed! They have the money and the power and the will and no confounded moral stamp is going to stop them from doing a blessed thing. Claiming anything else is nothing but wishful thinking of the most childish sort. To believe this is going to change anything.'

'It'll affect bank loans and various permits from the public sector and that will absolutely affect commerce. Stocks and bonds alike. Not to mention consumers.'

'And do you see what'll happen then? Those who have failed and lost business will go to the papers and tell their sob stories and try to explain why they are the way they are and then a massive part of the nation will fall all over themselves to support these people because they pity them and "man lives his best when he's on the mend". The whole thing is just one big, confounded farce.'

'But by the same token, the rest of us will also know who they are and can withhold our business, and they'll seek help and, hopefully, show some presence of mind,' says Óli. 'We're in the painful part. These are growing pains. Change is never easy.'

His father snorts.

'Imagine the future, five, maybe ten years from now,' Óli continues. 'When we're used to this new society in which people are like cars. They have to go in for inspection once a year so it's safe to send them out into traffic. If something's not working, then it needs to be fixed. As simple as that.'

'But people aren't cars, Óli.'

'We all have to answer to some greater law. Some mechanic.'

'Alright, son, have it your way. There's no talking to you, any more than to your sister.'

—

Tuesday passes in a fog. Óli forgets to eat. He jumps every time someone calls or messages him. He records a gram to send to the boy but deletes it. He scrawls out a statement to send to the media tomorrow, should the boy decide to turn down psychological treatment. He becomes more resentful with every passing hour. He resents the boy for his disrespect and resents himself for putting this in the boy's hands and resents Sólveig for backing him against a wall.

'How was your day?' asks Sólveig without interest when he gets home.

'The boy is not going to call,' he says, and it costs him something to maintain his composure.

Sólveig looks up: 'Are you still thinking about that?'

'Of course I'm still thinking about it.'

Sólveig is about to say something but Óli interrupts her: 'You know what? Don't answer that. We don't agree.'

He turns on his heel and locks himself in the bathroom before she can say anything, turns on the shower. He cranks the water up as hot as it will go until he can't stand it any more. When he opens the door, Sólveig has turned off the lights and is in bed.

Wednesday: forty-seven per cent in favour, forty-eight per cent against. Óli sits down in a locked office and calls the boy. He doesn't pick up. He's hiding. He's going to wait until after the vote. The boy is counting on his leniency. Just then, he looks through the glass wall and sees Salóme appear.

He opens the door a crack. 'Salóme,' he calls. 'Can I have a word with you?'

Two hours later, it's in all the biggest papers: photos of the slashed tyres and the red X on the front door and screenshots of the threats and the pictures he took through their window. Reporters call. Óli says he feels for the boy. He says he understands the boy, in a way. But understanding someone isn't the same thing as helping them. This just underscores the need for the new future they're fighting for. A future in which people like Tristan get real help.

At first, he feels like a great weight's been lifted off him. This isn't going to be a story. It'll just be one stone in a great cairn. But then he watches as the story rapidly climbs the Top Ten Most Read list. The news outlets say the boy has not been reached for comment. Óli doesn't expect that the boy or Magnús Geirsson will make a statement. He puts off going home for hours, grateful that he's back to taking his own car when Himnar says goodnight around ten. When he heads for home just after midnight, the story is the number-one most-read news item in the country. He silently undresses for bed and slips under the duvet. In the dim light of the bedroom, he can make out the shape of Sólveig's shoulder. She's awake.

Once, at a conference in the United States, he met a Canadian psychoanalyst who told him that, if parents didn't explain their struggles to their children, one day the children would unconsciously find themselves in similar or identical circumstances in order to try to make sense of what happened. They were all standing around a tall, circular table with glasses of prosecco and the psychoanalyst said it half-jokingly, in answer to something else. Óli laughed along with everyone else. To him, psychoanalysis was a subfield of literary studies, not psychology. But now, looking at Sólveig's shoulder, he could be looking at his mother's. One day, is Dagný going to ask the same questions that Óli did? Why hadn't her mother left him? Why did she put up with it, day after day, decade after decade? He reaches out in the darkness, kisses her shoulder before turning onto his back and closing his eyes.

He wakes up to ringing and fumbles for his headphones on the nightstand.

'Have you seen?' asks Himnar.

'Seen what?'

'The boy overdosed. The doctors aren't ruling out a suicide attempt.'

'What boy?'

'Tristan Máni.'

Óli sits up: 'Is he *dead*?'

'No, he's in an induced coma and on a respirator.'

'Jesus.'

'Yeah. Do you think you're up to coming back down to the office? The media's going to start calling.'

'Enough is enough,' says Magnús Geirsson on the afternoon news. 'The public needs to face up to the fact that the marking mandate is an ideal that just doesn't add up. Human lives are not a justifiable sacrifice for a false sense of security.'

'This is a terrible tragedy,' says Óli. 'We at the Icelandic Psychological Association send Tristan Máni our heartfelt wishes for a speedy recovery.'

'He was just angry,' says the boy's mother. 'He never would have done anything he said in those threats. He hated any kind of violence. He'd made the test into a much bigger deal than it was and wouldn't move to the Viðey Quarter with me no matter how I tried. He wanted to buy an apartment so he could live on his own terms.'

'We want an infrastructure that will catch these boys,' says Salóme. 'So that nothing like this happens again.'

The internet's on fire. Supporters says the mark could have prevented the boy's wretched fate. Critics blame Óli and the marking mandate, share Tristan's interview anywhere and everywhere. Óli sits in the conference room with his colleagues and they watch the discussion unfold. He's getting messages of all kinds – solidarity, encouragement, accusations, hatred.

Around two o'clock, the papers start reporting on a huge crowd of people streaming towards Austurvöllur Square.

'Thousands,' says the reporter. 'Drivers on the surrounding streets are laying on their horns. There are sirens going off everywhere, shouts and chants, some people are using their watches as megaphones. Two individuals have already been arrested for attempting to throw petrol bombs at Alþingi.'

Not long after, there's a *thunk* against the office window that faces the street. It takes Óli a moment to make out what's on the glass: streaks of egg and shell. They stand up and hurry to the front window. There aren't many people outside the building – four scruffy men and two women. They scream and ball their fists when Óli and his colleagues appear. This kind of thing has happened before. A small fraction of pro-testors wanders over here and gathers in front of the PSYCH headquarters, instead of going down to Austurvöllur.

One of them is holding a large, handmade sign. Anoth-er turns on the sirens. A middle-aged man flings his arm back, his face contorted with effort, and hurls another egg. It strikes the glass right in front of Salóme's nose and she jumps backwards. She calls the police immediately and then pro-ceeds to warn the other offices that have been working on the mandate campaign. The police tell them to lock all the doors and let no one in or out.

They move into the inner office and watch the news, trans-fixed, as the din outside the office gets louder. Óli calls Sólveig but she doesn't answer. He sends her a gram and explains the situation.

'Protesting isn't the solution,' says Magnús Geirsson. 'What's important now is to keep calm and exercise our right to vote on Saturday.'

'All available officers and SWAT teams have been called out,' says the National Police Commissioner.

The crowd in front of PSYCH's headquarters is growing. Óli estimates there are about thirty people. Himnar and Salóme take charge. Salóme is in direct contact with the police and Himnar is standing at the window, narrating what's happening outside. Around three o'clock, five police officers appear outside and try to disperse the mob, who simply move back from the entrance and continue to hurl abuse and eggs. Inside the office, they project two screens side by side: a major news publication on one, and the live feed from Austurvöllur on the other. Óli sees his own name and the name of the boy appearing over and over in the news coverage and comments.

But isn't *he* the victim here? *He* was the one who was threatened. Wasn't it his unequivocal duty to set the record straight when the boy played the innocent? How was he supposed to have foreseen that the boy would try to take his own life? On the live feed, an armed SWAT team stands guard in front of Alþingi. The horde spits, kicks. The din is a wall of sirens, chants, and shattering glass. Then the crowd hooks their arms together and tries to break through the SWAT line and force their way into parliament. The SWAT team is pushed back but then brace themselves against the wall with their feet, kick off, and shove the crowd back with their transparent shields.

Now and again another egg smacks the office window. Óli's colleagues shoot him sidelong glances.

A masked man steps forward and throws a green glass bottle through the window of an old timber-frame house right next to Alþingi. The mob screams in celebration and a second man follows suit, then a third. Moments later, black scarves of smoke ripple from the open wounds of the house. The SWAT team storms forward. A few of the officers cycle directly into the arsonists. Fierce fighting breaks out between the protesters and the SWAT team, getting worse by the second. Suddenly, a little canister appears from behind one of the shields and flies through the air. A thick, white fog streams from the canister. The mob retreats, shouting, sirens and screams echo over the square, someone trips backwards. The timber-frame house blazes in the background.

Tea,

I wasn't going to write back. I know you've got to have the last word so I'm not going to answer your next letter. If you want to see me, you can call. But for the past week, I haven't been able to think about you without getting absolutely furious. Angry enough that I want to end our friendship and never speak to you again. My psychologist says I ought to close the door on you, that our relationship has become toxic. That's just the way of it sometimes. But even if I'm furious, my psychologist's suggestion fills me with tremendous sorrow. To imagine a life in which I'm cut off from you, and you from me. The mere thought makes me think of all the bright spots we've had over the years – the friendship, the laughter, the warmth, the confidences and sense of security. Which makes me forget this present infection, the rivalry and jealousy, the power struggle. The things we've said. The brief, wounding comments that cut deeper and deeper with every passing year, every decade, until the infection's made its way into the bloodstream and turned deadly.

What is the value of a friendship? And to take it one step further: what is the value of a friendship that strips us of our masks? We no longer primp for one another. We've stopped donning our costumes. We don't plaster courteous smiles on our faces. We don't camouflage our feelings. We've crossed the threshold of intimacy into a space where there's no pretence, no screening. We've become two blobs of spit around one another, and we see ourselves reflected in the other's eyes and see the blob of spit that the other sees and it makes us feel like a blob of spit – it transforms us into blobs of spit. Which is why we start to hate ourselves when we're with each other. Because we don't want to be spit blobs. Until finally, we begin to hate each other for making us feel this way.

My mum has lost friends, too. Her best friend from childhood cut her off around the age we are now. When they met by chance at an outdoor event years later, under a twilit August sky, her friend walked straight up to her and embraced her. I love you, said her friend. I love you, too, said Mum. That was the only thing that passed between them. Then they continued on their way, each in their own direction. Mum cried when she told me this. She said: She knows me better than you do, Laíla. Every relationship in my life has its own laughter. My brother conjures a specific kind of laughter from me, and you conjure an entirely different laughter, and your father a third, my co-workers a fourth, my hiking club a fifth, and each laugh is as different as they are many. But sometimes, I feel like I lost my truest laughter when I lost her.

In spite of the aggression and the bitterness,

this is how I feel. Like I'm going to lose my truest laughter if I lose you. But then I think: Can we still laugh? Can we still conjure the brightest in one another? Therein lies the doubt, and grief, and infection. Part of me doesn't believe we can go back. That it isn't possible to reverse intimacy. For even if we don our costumes now, we'll still see the spit blobs underneath. You say something that offends me, and I reply with something that offends you and then we both leap into our defensive stances under the frankly farcical pretext that we're talking about the marking mandate.

Here's the lie of the land as far as I'm concerned: this isn't about politics. This is about our relationship. How you allow yourself to talk to me and I allow myself to talk to you. I've been flitting around the same questions for weeks. Whether – and if so, how – we can repair our friendship. Whether empathy is the key. I tried to imagine a future in which you'd utilise your understanding of me to figure out, in advance, if I'd be offended by something you were going to say. In which you'd start by thinking how you'd feel if I said the same thing to you, and then not say it. When I imagined this future, I could hardly believe how cruel and inconsiderate you often are. How frequently you say things that you yourself would be offended by.

And that's when it hit me. In my last letter, I

asked you to speak to me the way you speak to yourself. But now I see that's the problem: you do speak to me the way you speak to yourself. You scold me like you scold yourself. With unflinching cruelty and unstinting directness.

Dearest Tea. I don't know what the future holds. But I want to ask you one final thing: speak to me like I'm me. Keeping in mind that I will, in all likelihood, reflect your actions back at you. That I will answer cruelty with cruelty, attacks with counterattacks, and friendship with friendship.

I love you,
Laíla

24.

The curtains in the bedroom window are drawn, but she can sense that the sky outside is a polar blue. The sounds: aeroplanes, sparrows, the bright murmur of traffic. She hears Óli and Dagný in the kitchen, too: a spoon scooping from a bowl, a stool scraping the floor. She checks the time (eight-thirty), lifts her head just off the pillow, and projects the news in front of her: sixty-six people were arrested at the protest, four were seriously injured. She changes her mind, shuts off the projection, and gets out of bed. The bathroom is across the hall. She stands at the partially open door for a moment and then hurries silently across.

'Sólveig?'

She forces herself to look at him. It takes considerable effort to keep her expression neutral, her eyes empty. She knows that if her eyes give away her emotions, there will be no turning back: her cheeks will follow her eyes, her mouth will follow her cheeks, and her words will follow her mouth. In spite of everything, she is going to give him this one day.

'I'm going to resign on Monday,' he says. 'No matter how the referendum turns out tonight. I'm going to quit.'

She observes him. He's stressed. There's tension in his body, an entreaty in his eyes. Their daughter is watching a kids' show and wriggling distractedly in her seat, wearing nothing but a camisole, her back arched.

'I love you,' he says.

She opens the bathroom door and locks it behind her. Sits on the toilet, hides her face in her hands. Desire, she thinks to herself, is when longing and suffering combine.

He wasn't her type. She didn't generally let herself have crushes on guys whom all the girls had crushes on. And yet, from a distance she watched his reserved manner of speaking, his resolve. At night, she imagined him in her bed, holding her. In a cohort of just under two hundred people, it was clear that he was going wherever he wanted. He took an active part in all classes (which probably would have irritated her if she hadn't had such a crush on him) and at parties he'd talk incessantly, to anyone who could be bothered to listen, of the possibilities that the future held in store. It surprised no one when he ran for president of the psychology department's student association in junior year. It surprised no one that he went into politics with PSYCH when he finished his undergrad degree.

Women made up the majority of the clinic and Sólveig was not the only one enamoured of him. Not long before he started paying attention to her, she spent an hour at a party in a bedroom with a girl in their class who described all her interactions with him in great detail, imbuing the most unremarkable things with meaning – that he'd offered her a ride once (with two other people), that he'd laughed at her jokes and complimented her on an idea she'd had. The girl seemed to be on the border of hope and despair. Sólveig said nothing and decided (not for the first time) to stop thinking about Óli. The same night, she went home with some gangly medical student, as if to exorcise her desire with a different body.

To this day, she doubted that anything would have happened if she hadn't intentionally stopped looking at him. She sometimes imagines a long hallway lined with open doors and that, when she'd closed her door, that was when Óli became curious, knocked.

She dries off the body she's still getting used to, even though it's been three years since she gave birth. When the thought occurred to her a few weeks ago that she would (perhaps) have to premiere her body for someone new (in the distant future), her self-acceptance took many thousand steps back.

When she comes out, father and daughter have gone into the living room.

'I'll be back to take over around four,' she says from the vestibule.

'Where are you going?'

'To the office. I have an appointment with a patient.'

'What? On Saturday?'

'Yes.'

'What time will you be finished? I thought we could take our time getting all dressed up and then all go and vote together.' She can hear him trying to keep things light, positive.

'No, you two go together. I'll get down to the polling centre myself.'

In the beginning, she treaded carefully. When he invited her out, she held back, was careful not to give away too much, just the occasional breadcrumb here and there. He was both curious and attentive, asked insightful questions with tact, and Sólveig could see that he'd be a good psychologist. She found his ambition infectious, and his belief in the future. When he said he wanted to strengthen the weakest links in society, she wanted that, too. This was before she got to know those weakest links.

She tried to manage her expectations. He had a crush on her now, while she was a half-open door, but it wouldn't last unless she exercised a certain restraint. She knew this: desire feeds on distance. She never saw him two nights in a row (or hardly ever did); she was careful to see him in small doses, an average of six (eight) hours at a time; she didn't linger at his place after they spent the night together. He'd always try to keep her from leaving, would pull her back into bed. When he held her, fully dressed under the duvet, her whole body relaxed. She'd let herself lie there for a few minutes, until Óli dozed off and twitched, then she'd slip from his arms and creep out.

He made the first mention of moving in together after ten months, asked her again after eight more months. She took care with her excuses: she needed to focus on her studies (which was true – being in love was time-consuming); her lease was only for a single occupant; she wasn't ready. Her parents loved to psychoanalyse her in front of Óli, they finally had a co-conspirator. Every time the two of them went over for dinner, her parents explained, using examples from her childhood, that she needed a long time to think things over – she was a Capricorn, after all – and once asked him, laughing, what it was like for him, a Sagittarius, to be with such a calm and methodical person. He responded with questions: astrological signs were a bit like highlighters, wouldn't they agree? They emphasised a few sentences in a block of text. And weren't these rather unfair boxes to cram complicated and contradictory people into? On the way home from dinner that night, she asked him, in a moment of temporary insanity, to move in with her.

As soon as she gets in the car, she feels her face break into an ugly expression. She looks in the mirror: Just today and then it's over. She drives without thinking to where she'd said she was going, to her office. There's no appointment and Óli knows it. She buys herself breakfast at the coffeehouse at street level and takes it up with her. Then she flops onto the sofa in her office and eats and thinks.

Desire faded like hair dye, then gave way to intimacy. For the first five years that Sólveig worked as a psychologist, they were on the same team. The empathy test was a revolutionary method for determining whether a patient had a sense of cause and effect. It measured empathy and immorality, whether a person experienced a feeling of suffering or well-being when faced with the pain of others. There was an obvious correlation between certain characteristics. The less empathy a person had, the more likely they were to have a criminal record. It was an ultra-modern way to match up patients with medication and therapy, to measure recovery and results, and the correlation between results and antisocial behaviour. Sólveig shared her patients' insights (anonymised, of course) so that Óli could refine the infrastructure for the needs of the user. They came home and discussed solutions and ideas over dinner or red wine, sometimes with friends and family. When her father-in-law started to grouse and grumble, she took her husband's part. She liked being on the same team as Óli. He was good at debating.

She was having second thoughts when the discussion began about whether MPs should have to mark themselves. She understood the argument in favour of it, that those who tested below the minimum shouldn't be given such power. But it got on her nerves (though she didn't say as much) to see politicians and populists flaunting their empathy-test results in the media like certificates of their own merit. It proved nothing. It didn't disprove anything, either. Then Óli came home from work and told her about the Registry. She was thirty-four weeks along. She was tired and achy and couldn't believe she still had a month and a half left of her pregnancy. The idea gave her the creeps, but she tried to shake the feeling off. It was still just an idea. If it was carried out, a couple of thousand people would register, maybe. It would be a minor trend and few people would take any real notice of it. Nevertheless, she added her name to the list of signatories when several psychologists within PSYCH came out against the idea. Óli was hurt. But he respected her position (or at least said he did), that the empathy test was a tool that should only be used for a very circumscribed group of people, not as a stamp of quality or recommendation for the general public.

But then PSYCH established the Registry and people started marking themselves and marking spaces and companies jumped on the bandwagon and that creeping feeling she'd had got worse from day to day. Sólveig watched as several of her colleagues resigned from PSYCH and joined MASC and focused their energies on opposing the test. Óli didn't tell her about the marking mandate until a few days before the first bill was presented in parliament. It was a deliberate choice. He knew that she would put up obstacles. Which she did.

'There's nothing left,' she says out loud.

She projects her email. She has one unread message since yesterday.

Hello,

I'm a friend of Inga Lára's, she recommended you. I'm looking for a psychologist. Are you taking new patients?

Eyja E.

Sólveig types in the woman's name and sees that she's recently been outed in the media for failing the test. This is not uncommon. A person adjusts to changed circumstances. When outed individuals come to her for treatment, they want to be able to at least *say* they're working on themselves. It's an age-old social ritual: admit sins, receive grace. It will likely be a waste of time for the both of them. But she offers the woman an appointment next week. Then clicks off her holosystem, finishes her coffee, and decides to walk down to the polling centre.

She never complained (or very seldomly did) when he snuck to work while they were on parental leave. She said nothing when he worked at home with Dagný in his arms. Up until she stopped saying nothing and started complaining. At first, it was a stray grumble here and there, like farms dotted here and there out in the countryside. But then they increased, like a village gradually growing into a town. She couldn't control herself. She sat down with him and said, You have a child now. You have to be present, I feel like I'm steering this ship alone, and every single time, he made the effort, said, I'm sorry, love, this is so close to being over, as soon as we pass the bill, I'll take a real paternity leave. And things would get a little better for two, maybe three weeks. He'd turn off Zoé and pay more attention to his wife and daughter until the opposition played a new card and then they were forgotten yet again.

Desire returned, but it took a different form, distorted by anger and disappointment and resentment. The only time he called was to ask what was for dinner, whether she could pick Dagný up from playschool. When she told him he had to cook dinner three times a week, he still called on the way home to see what they had in the fridge, what he should make.

'You can figure that out yourself,' she said. 'You're a grown man.'

'But I'm just a Sagittarius, a lowly archer,' he answered, attempting a joke. 'You're the Capricorn, the resident goat of the household.'

Hundreds of cars are parked illegally all along the side of the road. On the street, the traffic jam inches forward, and people stream in and out of the polling centre. She runs into two old classmates on the way and a woman she can't place says hello. Probably a mother from the preschool. Or a patient who saw her once and then never came back.

She walks into the dark jaws of the gymnasium. An AI directs her to five people who are sitting at a long table, little cameras mounted on poles behind them. She gives her name, is given her ballot and directed to Hall F, where there's a short line in front of several voting booths.

Can she imagine more years spent slumped over on the border of hope and despair? No. Would it change anything if Óli did quit on Monday? No. The mark has cast a light on aspects of Óli's personality that she can't unsee, no matter how she might try. They've been highlighted, like key sentences in a many-hundred-page book: his self-centredness and self-justifications, his intolerance towards the flaws in humankind – not just behavioural patterns, but also those small, innocent things: nervous tics, noises, bad habits. The marking mandate is his way of dealing with his own intolerance. But you can't reprogramme people. You can't unravel people like old sweaters and reuse the yarn. She would give him tonight, but tomorrow she would take Dagný and go to her parents' house.

The booth smells of perfume and lipstick. Does she want this law to go into effect? No. She closes the envelope, walks out, and sticks it into the slot of the ballot box. When she releases it, she feels the way she does every time she's ever voted: that her vote doesn't make any difference, that the results will be exactly the same, with or without her.

25.

There's a clangour of celebration when the first projections are announced: fifty-nine per cent in favour, thirty-seven per cent opposed. Some whistle, some whoop, a round of clapping goes around the office. Then relief washes over the group in waves. Laughter, groans, sighs. The margin is greater than they'd ever dared hope for. Himnar slaps Óli on the back and Óli grabs onto Himnar to keep from falling. Hands are shaking. Knees are shaking. Óli's body is weak. Salóme goes out to talk to reporters. Moments later, her face appears on a giant screen, the office cheering in the background. Óli opens his first beer and the alcohol goes straight to his veins. He pictures rain in gutters. He lifts his glass with the rest of the committee, slaps a few backs and hugs a few bodies, drinks. He wishes that Sólveig were here with him. He wants to call her but knows better.

They're holding the watch party on the ground floor of their office, which young volunteers have decorated with fairy lights and gold pennants. The room is full of people dressed in their finest.

'This is nowhere near over,' he hears someone say. 'It isn't a done deal just yet.'

He finally notices how hungry he is. He looks around for

food and sees a long table at the back of the room with snacks and provisions. He slips through the crowd, fills a plate, and sits in the corner stuffing himself with canapés. He eats like he hasn't eaten in days.

When he's done, he sighs loudly and feels like he's coming back to himself. He calls Sólveig. She doesn't answer.

It isn't over, but he can't help getting swept up in the jubilation of the room. It's happening. They're building an actual welfare society. Everyone will get help. No one will be forgotten. Violence will be snuffed out at its first sign. He gets himself another beer and dives into the crowd. He spends a good, long time bouncing from a group standing here to another there. The newscaster says they should shortly have the latest projections and, for a moment, the room's attention sharpens, but then wanes with every newsless minute that passes. He tries to get a hold of Sólveig again, but it just keeps ringing.

Finally, he finds Himnar standing in a circle with four others.

'I feel like I'm coming back to earth,' says Óli.

'Me too,' says Himnar, grinning from ear to ear. They clink glasses. They chat with the others in the circle and discuss electoral districts and which ones have yet to report.

'It was that protest,' says one of the women in the circle then. 'That was the last nail in the coffin.'

'Yeah, or the violence of the protest,' says the man beside her. 'A protest in and of itself isn't a bad thing.'

'No, no,' says the woman. 'But you know what I mean.'

'You could actually say that this is all thanks to you, Óli,' says the man.

'I couldn't disagree with you more,' says Himnar. 'Óli was the victim of violence, both at the hands of Tristan and the protestors.'

'Yeah, of course, of course,' says the man. 'But he spoke out. Thankfully.'

The man lifts his bottle to Óli and drinks.

Óli stands in the group as long as he can. Then he excuses himself, steps into the stairwell, and sits on the stairs. A moment later, the door opens behind him. It's Himnar. 'Óli, you bear no responsibility for this.'

'I know.'

'*That boy* was violent towards *you*.'

'I know, Himnar.'

Himnar looks down at him.

'Still, I called the hospital today,' says Óli. 'The doctors say it's impossible to know whether he'll come out of the coma, and even if he does, what shape he'll be in.'

Himnar takes hold of his shoulder. 'It isn't your fault,' he says and prods him hard. 'There's nothing you can do about it. We'll think about it on Monday. Maybe we can help his family in some way. But it was the boy who made the choice to send you those threats and paint a distorted picture of himself. All of us would have gone to the papers with that. You did nothing wrong.'

Óli nods and swallows. He pictures the boy's face and his despair and the pills on his palm.

'Let's go back out,' says Himnar. 'There's nothing you can do now,' he says again. 'We have been working like dogs on this for years.'

'Give me a few minutes,' says Óli. 'I'm going to try to get a hold of Sólveig.'

Himnar purses his lips in assent. Then he pushes open the fire-escape door and returns to the gathering. As he does, another celebratory cheer erupts and echoes through the empty stairwell. 'Yesss!' someone cries out, right before the fire door closes on Himnar's heels.

26.

Tristan is in a pool. Sometimes, he dunks his head under. Sometimes, he chills out poolside. Then there's a blindingly sharp light. He hears the theme song for CityScrapers. He looks over at the lifeguard. He wants to play the game. He can hear the lifeguard talking somewhere.

'Hey!' he calls, but nothing happens.

'HEY!' he shouts, but no one hears him.

He hears a voice he knows and that's when he finally realises what is going on. He's inside his mum. He's a foetus again. He's stuck in her belly. He tries to move but all around him are soft, slimy walls and swollen organs. He feels slippery sausages that must be her intestines. He tries to squeeze them as a cry for help. He squeezes the sausages as hard as he can and hears his mum yelp. He loosens his grip a little. She knows he's there.

He opens his eyes and sees a white hallway. Or did he see the white hallway first and then open his eyes? He closes his eyes again. How old is he? Someone tells him. Someone tells him he's fifty years old.

Fuck. Has he really been here that long? He tries to open his eyes, but nothing happens. He tries and tries to open his eyes, but they refuse to fucking open.

He's in a prison camp during some old war. He's wearing green scrubs and he's tied to a chair. The general is also wearing green scrubs and wants to fight him. He'll unlock the chains if Tristan promises to fight him.

'I promise,' says Tristan.

He hears people on the other side of the wall. The wall is a little taller than he is. He jumps and jumps and jumps again. And finally, he opens his eyes. There's something in his mouth. A giant straw. He tries to swallow, but the straw is in the way.

'Zoé,' he says, but all that comes out is a muffled sound.

'Tristan?' says his mum.

'Sorry about the sausages,' says Tristan. Then he falls back asleep.

His eyes are open. His mum and his sister are sitting next to him. Naómí is talking. Her sweater is purple. Her words are like sweets that he tries to catch with an open mouth. But he can't seem to get them. They hit him in the face, and he doesn't like it, it's fucking annoying. He tries to open his mouth wider but the words keep landing on his face. On his cheek, then on his chin, then on his eyebrow.

—

They give him a cardboard box to eat.

'I don't want cardboard,' he says. 'Nei,' he says and tries to close his mouth. 'Cardboard boxes aren't food.'

He wakes up. The straw is gone. He has a terrible headache.

'Hi,' says his mum.

'Hi.'

He squints. There's junk all around her. Blankets and empty food containers.

'You're not that old.'

'No,' she says and laughs. 'I'm only fifty-one.'

'But if you're fifty-one . . .'

He doesn't understand. How could his mum be fifty-one if he's fifty? She couldn't have been a year old when she had him.

'Is this a hospital?'

'Yes, my love.'

'Why are we here?'

'Because of the trex, love.'

'Did I take too much?'

'Yes, my love.'

'How long have I been here?'

'Six days, my love.'

He searches his memory and finds nothing. The last thing he remembers was when he and Eldór went to meet that guy . . . that one guy. Magnús. Geirsson.

The second he remembers Magnús Geirsson's name, a new memory opens up, a memory of himself. And the old man on the S . . . who said 'ég hvet þig til dáða'. Told him to keep up the good work.

'What day is it?'

'The twenty-sixth of May.'

He looks straight at her.

'Is the vote . . . is the vote over?'

His mum frowns sadly and slowly nods her head.

'Did it pass?'

His mum nods again.

'Was I able to buy an apartment?'

'No, my love,' she says.

He closes his eyes. He wants to sleep some more.

'I'm fucking done for,' he says.

'Nei, don't say that, my love.'

'I wish I'd died.'

'My love, it's all going to be okay. We'll figure something out.'

He would never have believed how much lying in bed for a week could fuck you up. He gets out of breath just going to the toilet. He has trouble lifting his arms. The doctor says he needs to stay in the hospital for at least another week, but they're going to move him to a new ward. He has a bleeding ulcer in his stomach. A psychologist comes and asks if he has ever had suicidal thoughts.

'Nei,' says Tristan. 'I don't feel like I did this on purpose. But I obviously don't remember what happened.'

They give him pills that will supposably help with the

withdrawal. He hasn't gone so long without trex in years. He can't sleep at night and gets a sleeping pill from the night nurse. His whole body itches and he can't stop scratching.

Memories come to him in clusters. As soon as he remembers something little, he remembers all the stuff around the memory. It's like breaking the ice on a frozen puddle.

His mum tells him what happened the day after. Very slowly and calmly, like he's stupid or something. She tells him that Ólafur Tandri went to the papers with the threats, that there was a giant protest when everyone thought he was going to die. When he opens Zoé for the first time, tons of messages pop up from total strangers who say they are thinking of him or praying for him or standing with him. Sunneva says she can't believe it and she thinks about him every day and he means so much to her. His old friends from high school write long posts on social media where they share old memories of him from when they were little and say what a good friend he was and how nice and funny and fun to hang out with he was, but that he had his demons and the system failed him, and stuff like that. He can't stop fucking crying when he reads all that. He lies in the room alone and reads and reads and the tears just fucking stream down his cheeks. Rúrik posts updates about him and says that Tristan is the best friend he ever had and Tristan has always tried to do everything he can for him, even when he was acting like a fucking fool, and Tristan, bro, you better wake up, I fucking love you, man, you're the best fucking guy in the world.

When he can't cry any more, he turns off Zoé and lies there for a long time. Then he calls Rúrik.

Viktor sends him a gram and says he had to hire a guy to take his place. Tristan watches the gram a second time, and then a third, and he is so fucking happy and he's so fucking relieved and when he can keep a straight face, he records a gram to send back: he says he understands and no hard feelings.

His mum knocks on the door the next day. She's really happy, has this big smile on her face.

'I have news,' she says.

'Okay,' says Tristan.

'Okay, so, I was talking to Naómí's teacher this morning,' she says. 'She's this young woman who just quit her job at the school in the neighbourhood. She was actually apologising to me for a little thing that happened earlier this month but that's another story. I asked why she was quitting and she said she's going to focus on going back to school, that teaching was just an intermission, and then she said she was also going to sell her apartment, move somewhere else, she still doesn't know where. And wouldn't you know it, it's a little apartment for a single person or a couple, on the first floor, and the property valuation won't actually be all that high because the building isn't marked and there's a man on the third floor who doesn't want it to be marked while he's living there, he says he's going to die there. And so I told her about you and it turned out she'd seen the news and your video and

I asked if she might consider showing you her apartment and guess what?'

His mum beams.

'She said yes. We can go see it this week if we want. Before anyone else. And then I called the bank and asked about loan options and it turns out that if we make it look like I'm buying the apartment with you, that then I can get a loan that would be a little higher than yours, because I'm marked. You can just transfer me half of the down payment and then later, after maybe two or three years, we can transfer the title to you, and you can refinance.'

His mum looks at him with a hopeful smile now, her eyebrows raised.

'Já . . .' he says. 'But I still have to take that test either way.'

His mum looks at him.

'I think I'm going to just go ASAP and see if I pass,' he says. 'If I don't pass, then maybe we try that. If I do pass, though, then I was thinking maybe I could move home into that bedroom that you were telling me about. Then I wouldn't have to work and go to school at the same time and all that.'

His mum starts crying and Tristan lets her hug him.

The halls are white and the floor is light blue. Everything smells like rubber and hand sanitiser. A nurse walks in front to show them the way through the hospital. Her shoes squeak. His mum walks next to him. They turn and turn and walk down long hallways and then they come to a white waiting room.

Good morning, says an AI at reception. *Please take a seat. The doctor will be here presently.*

They sit down and the nurse who showed them the way turns to them.

'It's no big deal,' she tells Tristan.

Tristan nods and the nurse leaves. He thought he'd be literally so fucking stressed but he just feels flat. The psychologist said the new meds he's taking to get off the trex would do that, but that they wouldn't affect how he does on the test. He and his mum sit alone in the waiting room for a little while and then a dude around Tristan's age comes in and sits down across from them. A door opens and some guy in scrubs sticks his head out.

'Tristan?'

'It's going to be fine,' says his mum. Tristan nods and stands up.

'Welcome,' says the guy in scrubs and holds the door open for him.

They walk through a little room and into another room. There's a chair and a big helmet with straps. Tristan sits in the chair and the guy fastens the straps and rubs some spray into his hair and then puts the helmet on his head. All of a sudden, Tristan thinks about Sunneva. She'll have to take the test, too. Maybe, when this is over, he can write to her and invite her out on a real date. Maybe she'll be his girlfriend. Maybe.

'Have you taken the test before, Tristan?' asks the guy.

'No.'

'We're going to play a few videos for you and you don't have to do anything but watch them. Here is a button if you start feeling claustrophobic or if you need to take a break.'

'Okay.'

'Great,' says the guy and smiles at him. 'Everything's going to be just fine.'